THE
BROKEN

BY

KER DUKEY

The Broken
Copyright © 2013 Ker Dukey
Published by Ker Dukey

Editor: Kyra Lennon @ Black Firefly
Proofreader: TJ Loveless @ Black Firefly
Cover by Ari @ Cover it! Designs
Formatted by Black Firefly
www.blackfirefly.com

DEDICATION

This book is for my sister Leah. Thank you for giving me the courage to put my book out there, for loving everything I write.
To the readers who embrace the characters and lose themselves in the story thank you.

PROLOGUE

River

It's the night of my sixteenth birthday, sweet sixteen. Everyone's sixteenth should be memorable. Mine will be, just not for the right reasons.

Sammy's hands are touching my skin, his breath on my neck, and his words in my ear. He's my brother's best friend, and our next door neighbour. He's the same age as my brother, two years older than me, and he has always been my first and only crush. I've felt things for him since the first day I laid eyes on his dark, unruly hair and soul-warming blue eyes. His smile is sweet; his laugh gives me goose bumps. His eyes light up whenever I enter a room and I know he feels the same way about me. He used to call me Twinkle Toes because I'm a dancer, and as I got older, Twinkle Toes became just Twink. He's who I feel inside me, taking my virginity. He's loving me, caressing my skin, giving me that special first time all girls should have. He looks into my eyes, tells me how beautiful I am, how much he loves me. He is who I feel sliding his length in and out of my sacred place.

"I love you so much, you know that right? You owe me this, River."

His words break through my daydream, Sammy's image fades, and Danny's takes its place. His tears drip into my neck, itching my skin; his fingers slightly pinching the skin on my cheek as he holds my face to one side. His heavy body weights me down, pinning me to my small childhood twin bed. A burning sensation and a sharp stabbing pain assaults me as he thrusts inside me. I hold back my screams, swallow them down, burying them, but I'm worried if I hold the tears in they will flow inside me, drowning me, and so I let them flow from my eyes. My pillow soaks them into its soft plump fibre; the pillow that usually offers me comfort at night will now forever hold the tears from my stolen innocence. He thrusts harder and grunts before his body relaxes and I feel more of his weight press against my small frame, making it hard for me to breath. He's still muddy from the garden; it's dirtied my sheets and nighty. He grips my chin and forces me to look into his dark brown eyes. "You belong to me. What I did for you and your brother, I'll never tell anyone if you admit you belong to me and that you wanted this."

I force down the lump in my throat and ask him why he's crying. His eyes narrow. "Because I love you and you just gave me something beautiful, now say you belong to me." He growls the last words, his grip tightening on my chin. "I…I…belong …to…y…you," I stutter.

He grins and lifts from my body. There's a burning ache between my thighs. I wait for my door to close behind him as he leaves before I pull my knees up to my chest and roll into the fetus position. I cry, broken. I cry for my brother, I cry for my father, I cry for my stolen innocence, and I cry for Sammy. I was meant for him.

FOUR YEARS LATER

River

I'm lying, looking at the ceiling, going over the grocery list in my mind. Danny is telling me he loves me as he thrusts inside me. I feel my body moving, but I'm numb and his words sound distant. I moan on cue; it's built into me and I don't even notice when I'm doing it anymore. When his weight shifts off me, I get up from the bed and head for the shower. I turn the tap, wait for the splutter, and then the water flows like rain. I check the temperature and slip under the warm stream. It pitter-pats over my skin and I close my eyes, relaxing into the flow of water.

"You're so beautiful, River. I hate that other men get to look at you."

I startle at the sound of Danny's voice. I didn't realise he followed me in here. It's his calm voice; his thinking too much voice. My heart rate increases, there's a slight tremor in my hands. He has such a dominating, dark presence for someone of only twenty two years old, like he's lived more lifetimes before this one.

"I'm yours, Danny," I tell him.

There's a slight break in my voice. I get nervous when he's like this. This could end with him proving to me I belong to him.

"Tell me you love me, Riv."

My stomach drops. I need to be so careful and make my voice sound strong. I open my lips, taking in some of the water trickling down my face to moisten my dry mouth. "I love you, Danny."

He scrubs his hands down his face and lets out a shaky breath.

"I love you too, so much."

He steps into the shower and pulls me into him; I'm crushed against his chest, his strong arms squeezing me so tight my ribs hurt. He stays with me like that until the water turns cold.

I dress in jean shorts and a white t-shirt. It pulls slightly tight at my breasts, like most of my tops, and leaves a small slither of navel showing. My body is not that of a typical dancer. I have a D cup bust and a small toned waist, which only magnifies my large chest. Although I have a small waist, I have hips and too much ass; most people tell me I'm lucky to have my figure, but they aren't the ones who struggle for clothes to fit right.

"Hey, sis," Blaydon calls as I enter the kitchen. He's sitting at the old wooden breakfast table that has so many scratches and dents it looks like it's been dragged out of a wood chipper and glued back together. His eyes come up to mine as he continues pushing cereal around a bowl, but not eating any. He has dark circles under his eyes, his overgrown shaggy blonde hair tucked behind his ear needs a comb, and he looks worn out. I walk up behind him and slip my arms around his shoulders, my cheek resting on his head. "You have trouble sleeping last night?"

He pats my arms and half smiles. "Don't I always?" The sadness in his voice breaks my heart. "Is Danny here?"

I release my hold on him and smile, its fake but he never notices. I point down the hall to Danny coming out of my room. He locks eyes with Blaydon as he saunters into the kitchen. "You low again?" Danny asks Blay with a raised eyebrow. Blay drops his head, shoulders slumping in defeat.

"Yeah, I went to a party last night, shared with Maria."

Danny shakes his head in frustration. "She's always fucking using you for your drugs, Blay. Cut the bitch loose, this is the last time I give you extra. We can't afford to supply that bitch's habit as well as yours." Blaydon exhales hard and looks up to Danny.

"I know, man, I've cut her loose, I told her."

I watch as Danny pulls out a small clear bag from his jeans. It has pills inside, and he slides it across the table to Blaydon. My heart constricts when Blay grabs at it like its water in a desert. I slip around Danny and head outside for the mail.

The summer heat hits me as soon as I step off the porch; I feel the kiss of the sun on my skin. I close my eyes and pretend I'm somewhere else; a meadow, clear crystal blue skies the same colour as Sammy's eyes.

"Damn, you're a fine piece," I hear a male voice say. I open my eyes and look over at Sammy's house. He hasn't lived there for four years, but to me it will always be Sammy's house. Jase, Sammy's nine-year-old brother, is sitting on the steps leading to their porch. A guy holding a bottle of Jack Daniels is leaning against the pillar at the top of the steps. I walk over and he ogles me like a sex starved pervert in a brothel. "Hey, sugar. Want to come party?" he croons, offering me the half empty bottle of Jack.

I grimace and shudder. "God, no."

My eyes travel over his unkempt, black, greasy hair. He has small, beady eyes and he's wearing last night's clothes. I can tell because they're crumpled and have a few stains slopped down the front. I look down to Jase. He's in his PJs, his blonde messed-up mop in disarray on top of his head. He looks tired. He could pass as a young Blay, and if I didn't know better, I would say he's Blay's kid. "Hey, buddy. What are you doing out here like that?" I point to his outfit.

He shrugs. "Mom locked me out while she speaks to her friend. She's taking ages."

I look up at the creeper staring at my t-shirt like he has X-ray vision and stamp up steps. "How long has he been out here? And why are you out here?"

His filthy eyes trail down my body and back up, and he licks his lips. "She's just seeing to my friend. He knows her or some shit; I'm just waiting for him."

I turn to Jase. "Have you had breakfast?"

He shakes his head. I look at my watch, it's a little after twelve.

"Blay's inside having breakfast. Why don't you go in there and get him to make you some?"

Jase jumps up and runs off into my house. I wait for my front door to close behind him before I wrap my knuckles hard against the door.

"Sandra, open this door!" I screech as my knuckles begin a steady thump on the wood. Creepy guy reaches for me, his hand brushing down my back.

"Come on, sugar. Leave them be, you can keep me company."

I bat his hand away. "Don't fucking touch me."

He steps closer. "Come on, don't be like that, sugar."

I glare at him, daring him to touch me again. He reaches and grabs my ass. "Keep your fucking hands of me, creep!" I slap him across the face so he stumbles back.

"You fucking bitch!" He steps towards me. I see movement in my peripheral vision, but I'm too pissed off to look to see who it is. Only Danny gets to touch me and talk to me how he wants, because I owe him. He owns me, so to make up for having to submit such a big part of who I am to Danny, I refuse to take shit from anyone else. I pull my arm back and crack him right on the nose. It hurts like a bitch, but when I see his blood trickle from his nostril, I smile. He lunges at me, and I see a blur of movement, then feel hands on my hips and a body blocking my view. He's saying things in a calming voice like I'm a scared child; did he not see me punch that creep? I start to speak when the figure from behind him comes into view. My heart skips, then pounds erratically. I look down, sure I'll see it beating out of my chest. I'm holding my breath, memories storm my brain, crashing through me like a tornado, twisting and pulling at every emotion, leaving me a mess.

"Breathe for me Twink."

Sammy!

CHAPTER ONE
Sammy

Slipping out of bed and into a pair of jeans, I rub my temples. My head is throbbing from overdoing it at the bar last night. I check the clock and groan. It's seven a.m. and I should be on the road by now. I'm hoping the chick I brought home and left naked and satisfied on the couch has fucked off already. I run my fingers through my messy bedhead and saunter into the hall, hearing the sound of someone moaning. Rolling my eyes, I follow the sound into the living room. My roommate is lying on the couch with the chick I brought home, and she's riding his dick enthusiastically. "Oh my God," she screeches when she sees me. "You're who I came here with?" She poses it as a question, but it's a statement. I raise an eyebrow and look down to Jasper. He grins. "Hey bro, coffee's brewing. Found this naked chick on the couch."

She gasps, her hand slapping across Jasper's face and I grimace from the sound.

"What the fuck?" he bellows.

She lifts off him and searches for her clothes. "You son of a bitch! You asked me if I wanted to keep the party going when I woke up to find you naked beside me. I assumed it was you I came here with."

Jasper looks to me, then at the irate women pulling on her panties. "She fucking serious?" He laughs then sits up. "You don't even remember who you came home with! You climbed up on my dick without question, and then have the audacity to act offended at me! My dick should be offended I let your second hand pussy anywhere near it! Now, are you going or climb back on or what?"

Her mouth is agape and she's holding her skirt in her hand as she stands and stares at Jasper. She then turns her focus on me with a question in her eyes. I laugh and shake my head. "Don't look at me, I don't even remember your name."

She huffs and squints her eyes. "You're both assholes," she growls, heading for the front door, which she exits, still holding her skirt.

"Man, these fucking bar sluts act like whores then moan if you treat them like one," Jasper says, frustrated. He looks down to his still hard cock and then at me and grins. "I'm going to take a shower then I'll be ready to go home with you."

I shake my head and go to pour a much needed coffee.

As I watch the miles count down, bringing me closer and closer to my childhood home, my thoughts are all of River. We had an unspoken connection between us; well, at least I thought we did. I was her brother's best friend so I had to keep my feelings for her a secret. I was waiting for her to turn sixteen, than I planned to speak to Blaydon. Let him know I loved his sister, always had, ever since I first saw her eye peering at me through a hole in the fence. She made life better for me. When my mom would drink herself into a stupor, she would make sure I ate. She would do my laundry so I didn't have to wear dirty clothes to school, she looked out for me and showed me affection when my own fucking mother couldn't. She was so gorgeous, too. Long blonde hair with darker shades running through it. Her eyes were the colour of the ocean on one of those hot as fuck islands, bright green, that you just want to swim in. Her body was lean and shapely. She had always had large tits and she hated it. She had no idea how much girls envied her, and how badly all the guys wanted her. She was stunning and she never knew it. She was intoxicating, in a good way. I would happily lose myself in everything River was. Her scent made me want to inhale every time she got close.

She smelt sweet, like cocoa. Her smile made my stomach twist, her lips were so red and full. Her laughter made me lightheaded as it swam around, echoing in my mind. Her small subtle touches made my skin vibrate with need and when she danced, she owned me, sucked me in and consumed me. Her sixteenth birthday happened on a weekend I had to stay with my dad and little brother, so I went shopping for her gift and planned to give it to her when I got home the day after. It was a promise ring. She was it for me; my soul mate, I lived not on air, food or water, I lived on *her*. I breathed her, I drank her in and consumed her with every look.

When I got home, my heart was shredded. Danny, mine and Blay's close friend, had swooped in, taking what was meant for me. My soul wept that day and I've never let myself hurt like that since. I turned my heart to stone. I watched my mother break my dad's heart over and over through the years, and when my solace, my River, broke mine, I vowed to never let a women touch that part of me again. I never understood why she chose him and I couldn't stick around to watch them together. I left for college and never came back, until today.

⚡⚡⚡

"So are you going to take me out tonight, and show me what the pussy's like in this home town of yours?" Jasper grins at me.

I grip the steering wheel tighter as River's image flashes in my mind again. She was only sixteen when I last saw her, an innocent beauty. "We can't, I told you. My dad dropped Jase off yesterday, and we need to watch him for a few days while my dad's away with his new wife."

"Isn't that what your mother's for?"

I glare at him briefly then turn my eyes back to the road. The familiar scenery fills my eyesight; old wooden houses all shapes and sizes, paint chipping on some. Mr Black's house is still an awful bright yellow. Who paints their house brighter than the sun? I'm sure that fucker could be seen from space.

I slow the car to a coasting roll. "I told you, my mother didn't earn that title, she's a fucking drunk, who will more than likely never be home because she's too busy fucking anyone and everyone who is willing to put his dick in her."

Jasper grimaces. He's as crude they come, so I know my description of my mom was maybe a little too crass if he got offended by it.

"Ohh, check those legs out," Jasper says, bringing my attention to a man at my front door trying to grope...fuck me, it's River.

I stop the car and jump out. Jasper looks surprised but follows my retreating frame up the garden path.

"Keep your fucking hands of me, creep!" she shouts, and slaps him across his cheek so he stumbles back.

"You fucking bitch," he shouts back at her, stepping into her personal space. I'm just about to leap at him when she pulls her arm back and punches him square on the nose. There's a crack, and then blood trickles down his face and over his lip. He lunges forward, but I jump up the stairs and tackle him before he can make contact. I rain a few blows down on him, two to the face, and three to the ribs. I go to land another to his face when I realise his body is limp, he's out cold. I jump up to find Jasper with his hands on River's hips, crouching down to get in her eye line and talking to her soothingly. "Are you okay, sweetheart? Do you know this douche bag?"

Her eyes find mine and she stops breathing. I watch as her chest stills, her mouth is open in an O shape, a thousand emotions play across her eyes. I walk closer to her, leaning over Jasper's shoulder.

"Breathe for me, Twink."

She gasps, taking in a lungful of air. "Sammy."

"Get your fucking hands off her! Now!"

We all turn to see Danny tearing across the lawn. He leaps the stairs and shoves Jasper away from River, pulling her behind him. She rests her hand on his shoulder. "It's okay, Danny."

He turns and glares at her. She flinches and I see fear burn in her eyes for a brief moment. My body goes tense.

"Chill the fuck out man, we were helping her out," Jasper shouts, puffing his chest out at Danny. Danny's eyes bore into Jasper like he could kill him with a stare alone. "That douche got a little hands-on, so we stopped to help her out." Danny's eyes flash to the bleeding mess on the floor and I watch as anger then pure rage takes over his features. His hands begin to shake. I've known Danny a long time. He was always a little scary. His dad liked to take his fists to him often, that's why Blay took a liking to him, they had that in common. Danny is hardened; he knows how to take a beating, making him outlast any opponent in high school, and then with age, came size and experience. One day his dad took his fist to him, and he gave his fist right back, leaving his dad in the hospital for a week.

"Danny, I took care of him."

His eyes shoot to mine and recognition flashes in them. "Sam?"

"Hey man, I told Blay I was coming. Did he not tell you?"

Danny shakes his head and body like he's ridding himself of his coat of anger. "Yeah, he told me."

River's mouth pops open again as her eyes bore into the side of Danny's head. I'm guessing no one told *her* I was coming home.

The front door opens and an older looking guy steps out and stops abruptly. His hands are on his belt, he's buckling it up. My mom stands behind him in a robe. I glare at him, then her.

"Sammy, what are you doing here?" she says, surprised.

"I fucking live here. Dad signed the house over to me. Where the fuck is Jase? So help me, Mother, if he's in there listening to that shit!"

Her face goes white. "You and that prick of a father conspiring against me! This is my house, Sammy."

River steps forward and looks at me. "Jase is at mine, Sammy." She turns to my mother. "You disgust me, Sandra." My mother steps back holding her chest, acting offended, but River isn't finished. "You have that boy once in a blue fucking moon and I find him out here, in his PJs with some creep!"

"Oh, save the saint act, you little tart." My mom sneers at River.

Danny's finger shoots out, pointing right in my mother face. "Watch your fucking mouth, you stupid bitch."

"Sammy?" Jase's voice comes from behind me; we all turn to see him standing with Blaydon.

"What's going on?" Blaydon asks.

"Nothing," Danny informs him, grabbing River by the wrist and pulling her down the stairs, across the lawn, and into their house.

"I can't believe you let someone talk to your mother like that," Mom snaps.

"Start acting like a mother and I'll act like your son."

I turn to Jase and grin. "Hey, buddy! Guess what I brought?"

His face lights up. "Your X-Box?"

I laugh. "Yeah, man. Let's unpack and you can show me your skills."

CHAPTER TWO

River

Danny pulls me across the lawn and into the house. "What the fuck happened over there?"

I flinch from the aggression steaming from him. "Some creep waiting for Sandra was drunk and being -" My voice is cut off when Danny's hands wrap around my throat, his body pushing flush with mine, his lips panting against my ear. "You should have been nowhere near him, River. What the fuck?"

I try to swallow the lump in my throat, but his grip is too strong. He inhales sharply. "That other guy had his hands all over you, and you let him, River."

I try to shake my head, but he has me completely immobile in his grasp. I hear voices, and Danny's hands loosen and slide into my hair. "Go take a shower and wash off his hands. You're mine, River."

A single tear slips free from my eye, creating a wet path down my cheek. The front door swings open and Blaydon enters.

"What's going on Riv? What happened with that guy?" he asks, then comes closer and sees my tear. He reaches for me, pulling me from Danny. "What's wrong, Riv? Did the asshole hurt you?"

I shake my head. "Sammy stopped him," I croak, my voice hoarse, my throat scratchy. I look over to Danny. He has a snarl contorting his features. He's angry still and I begin to shake.

"You're trembling," Blay states, crushing his body to mine. "I would kill anyone who hurt you."

I grimace, and he pales at his words and my reaction.

"Go shower, River," Danny commands. I pull away from Blaydon and smile weakly at him. Running my hand down his arm, I turn and to go shower for the second time today.

I pull on my black dance leggings and sports top, tying my hair into a tight bun and when I open the bedroom door, I come face to face with Danny. He looks remorseful, his brow furrowed, eyes apologetic. I step back as he steps forward. Closing the gap between us, he cups my jaw, his touch soft and gentle. "I'm sorry about earlier," he breathes, and I let out the breath I was holding. "You know it makes me crazy when guys touch you, River. I just love you so much. " He nuzzles his lips into my neck. "I'm going away for a few days for business and it's been playing on my mind. I don't like leaving you."

I reach up to stroke the back of his head. "It's okay. I'll be here waiting for you."

He strokes my cheek and brings his lips to shower kisses on my own. I swallow the bitter bile in my throat and return his touch.

"Tell me who you belong to, River." His voice has taken on an edge I'm all too familiar with. His hand slides from my cheek to grasp the nape of my neck, my forehead being tipped forward to rest against his.

"I belong to you, Danny," I tell him, only a slight tremor in my voice. I know why he needs to hear me say these things. I've woken up to him sitting in the chair in our room, mumbling things his parents used to tell him; he's nobody, no one will ever love him, he doesn't belong, he's poison.

He pulls away and smiles before leaving. I exhale and inhale a few times, trying to compose myself before I open the bedroom door. I walk through the house to the garden.

Breathing in the fresh air, I walk up the three steps to the raised decking platform Blaydon had built for me to dance on. I slip my earphones in, clip my iPod inside my bra, and I let Adele sing her soul into my ears and take over my body.

CHAPTER THREE
Sammy

The house hasn't changed since I left. The walls are still painted light green, the dark furniture is still the same beaten down furniture we always had, and the stale smell of cigarettes is stagnant in the air. The wood flooring looks a little worse for wear, but I'm not surprised. Blay informed me that mom likes to have parties most weekends.

In my old room, memories assault me at the sight of my bed. My mind floods with visions of River sleeping there. When her mom killed herself, River used to have nightmares. If Blay wasn't home, she would sneak across the yard and sleep in my bed. I prayed for those moments with her, to lie next to her breathing in her air, her scent.

God, I've been home five minutes and I'm already growing a vagina over her, but fuck, she's still stunning. More so. I drop my bags down and take in the familiarity of my room. Nothing has changed, even down to the blue bedspread and drapes. The checked wallpaper reminds me of the film *American Pie;* Jim's room suffered the same wallpaper. My old Mustang posters bring a smile to my face. That was a dream of mine and Blay's. We wanted to find and restore old muscle cars in the garage once we bought it from his dad. It's crazy to walk back into a life you ran from.

Jase is a little ass kicker on *Call of Duty*, he's currently leading on the score board and putting Jasper to shame. I gave up a while ago to raid the fridge for sustenance. The only thing in the fridge is a pack of expired eggs. I grumble, knowing I need to get some shopping in. I hate going to the supermarket.

A shadow catches my eye out the window; I walk over and nose out to see River dancing on a raised platform in her backyard. God, she's breathtaking. The way her body moves is incredible.

"What you looking at?" Jasper's voice penetrates my ears. He looks out and groans. I shoot my elbow back into his stomach. He makes a pained noise and then slaps me around the head. "What the fuck?"

I turn to face him. "She's taken."

He raises an eyebrow. "And?"

"Her brother and boyfriend are my friends, so she's off limits, Jasper."

"Seriously Sammy? Because she is so fine. Fuck, have you seen that body?" He leans over me to watch her again and I swallow the growl I want to let rip from my throat. He looks back at me, and reading my expression, holds his hands up. "Fine, off limits. I get it."

"We need food, the house is empty," I tell him, changing the subject.

"Okay, well you do a store run and I'll stay with the kid."

I pat my pockets to make sure I have my wallet and car keys, and walk back to the living room. "Jase, I'm away to the store. Look after Jasper for me, okay?" Jasper slaps me in the back of the head again before throwing himself onto the couch and picking up the controller. Jase nods and gives me a quick wave, too involved in the game to care. I open the door and catch

Danny's eye as I walk down the path. His carrying a duffle bag and laptop case.

"Where are you off to?" I ask.

"Work. I'll be gone a few days," he answers, sounding deflated.

"What are you doing these days? Still a whizz on the computers?" I ask with a grin he returns with one of his own.

"Yeah, I work with the old man selling computer programs. It's a new business but it's going well and I'll be bringing in the big bucks soon enough."

I laugh, shaking my head. "Still planning on being a rich son of a bitch, then?"

Danny had always said he would be rich and buy a paradise island to live on when he got older. Blaydon and I had always worked at the garage Blaydon's dad owned. The plan was for me to do a business course at college and buy his dad out with some inheritance I have from my gran passing when I was younger. Then Blay and I would run it together; me the business side, him the grafting side, as his dad was never there anyway. Too busy drinking his weight in whiskey down the local rat hole.

"Yeah, I plan on setting up the business then reaping the rewards while other fuckers do the slack work, but I need to get the foundation laid first." He grins. I give Danny his due. He's clued in when it comes to computers. That shit just comes to him naturally. What surprises me is him saying he's in business with his old man. Danny hates his dad and vice versa. It's no secret they have an abusive relationship. Danny had got drunk one night with me and Blay after he got into a fight with his dad, and was sporting a black eye. He rambled on and on about his dad hating him. Apparently, his dad gave up a big time deal to play football because Danny's mom got pregnant at seventeen, so he married her and took a job at some shitty accounting firm, only to later learn Danny wasn't his.

"So, how's Blay doing? He looks strung out," I say, slightly afraid of his reply. Blay looks older than his twenty-two years. He's too slim and withdrawn; clearly on drugs.

Danny looks up to the house then back at me. "He's dependent on anti-depressants." His eyes search mine but I'm not sure what he's looking for.

"What the fuck? Since when?"

He runs a hand through his hair. "Since their dad did a runner."

My stomach drops. Fuck, their dad was a waste of space. He couldn't cope when his wife killed herself when River was twelve, and turned to drink and beating Blaydon to cope. To have both parents abandon you in their own ways must have taken its toll. Fuck, we all had shit luck in the parent lottery; between us I think the only half decent parent is my dad, and even he struggles to show real affection. My mind goes to River, her beautiful spirit. How could anyone want to leave her?

"What you looking at?" Danny's voice breaks me from my musing, and I realise I'm looking to the back gate that leads to where River is dancing. "Nothing, sorry. I was just lost in memory lane. So when did he leave?"

Danny furrows his brow. "River's sixteenth." He raises an eyebrow like I should have known this, but I didn't. I left a couple days after her birthday. I couldn't watch her be with anyone who wasn't me.

"Has he been in touch or anything?"

I see something flash across Danny's face, but I can't put my finger on what it is.

"No, he's gone." He says it with such finality. I look back at the house. "How's River been?"

I watch his jaw tic with tension. "She has me. I look after her."

I nod and offer a weak smile. "We should have a party when you're back, and Jase is back with my dad. A reunion party." I grin and he returns it.

"Sounds good."

We say our goodbyes and go to our separate cars.

The supermarket is empty, much to my pleasure. I hate trolley rammers and queues. I throw in some random shit; eggs, cereal, bread, meat, juice, sodas. I get to the beer fridge and collide with a petite blonde; her dainty frame falls back and hits the glass door of the fridge.

"Fuck! Sorry, sweetheart." I grab her arm and steady her.

She looks up at me and her familiar brown eyes dance with excitement. "Sam!" she screeches and jumps, throwing her arms around my neck, her legs around my waist. "Hey stranger!" She breathes in my face, her intoxicated breath making me pull away.

"Chelsea, you smell like a brewery." I slide her to her feet.

"I may have been drinking," she slurs.

"You think?" I cock an eyebrow and she giggles.

"God Sam, you haven't changed one bit. Look at you." She bites on her bottom lip and roams her eyes up my body shamelessly. "How was college?"

"Good," I say, watching her shift from foot to foot. She's practically panting. I could probably take her up against the fridge right now if I wanted.

She steps forward and runs a hand down my chest. "Girlfriend?" she asks, and I laugh at how blatantly obvious she's being. We hooked up in school; she was a slut and wasn't shy about being passed around at parties. I look her up and down. She's still hot; she has a tight little body. She's lacking in the tits department, but she makes up for it by being filthy.

"No girlfriend, Chels."

She beams and slides her body closer. I feel the heat coming off her and I grin back. "Why don't you stop by tomorrow? My aunt's picking my brother up in the morning, we can catch up."

She bites her lip. "Mmm, sounds good."

I watch her saunter away up one of the aisles. Shaking my head in disbelief at how easy she still is, I open the fridge and grab a couple of six packs, before making my way to the cashier.

When I get back, I find Jasper leaning up against the counter talking to River, who's at the stove, stirring a sauce that smells fucking divine.

"Hey, look who came over to cook for us. Your mother left, by the way, and be glad you weren't here to see what she was wearing… or not wearing." Jasper shudders.

River shakes her head. "Actually, I just came to get you started. I wanted to make sure Jase has a real meal and not," she puts down her spoon and walks over to me, peering her head into my shopping bag, "beer or cereal for his dinner."

She lifts one perfect brow at me, and I just stand there, taking in her presence and her scent. Fuck me, I still want her. After all this time, I still want to wrap her in my arms. Fuck. I hate that I still want her when she chose Danny over me. She chose him, and now she's standing in my kitchen, telling me how to take care of my own fucking brother.

"Actually, I'm taking him out to eat," I snap and she looks at me, confused by my bitter tone.

"Oh, I'm sorry, Sammy. I was only playing about the beer and cereal. I know you can look after him," she stutters and I feel like a dick. "You can use this tomorrow, then. It will keep."

I look over at the pot and grimace. She sees my face and fire ignites behind her eyes.

"Nah, you can just bin it or take it home with you," I tell her, to see if the fire she used to have is really still in there. In all honestly, I'm not taking Jase out, I'm going to order pizza, and I'm praying she leaves her sauce here because I've missed her amazing cooking. She looks at Jasper and smiles, scooping some sauce onto the spoon and holding it out to him. The traitor, kiss-ass, bastard opens his mouth and sucks the spoon clean, and then groans. She looks at me and dips the spoon back into the sauce. Collecting a big spoonful, she walks over to me holding it at my lips. "Open your mouth, Sammy," she commands, and I smirk. She shoves the spoon into my mouth, it clinks against my teeth as I taste what she's offered, and it's delicious. She pulls the spoon from my mouth and brings a finger to the corner of my lips, sweeping at some sauce that escaped. I watch as she brings the finger to her mouth and sucks it. I swear my dick shot up to attention and a small growl left my lips.

"Mmm, tastes fantastic, just like I always knew it would," she moans, and I feel my body humming with need.

"Oh God, that's hot." Jasper groans, pulling River's attention from me.

She chuckles and pats his chest. "Leave the sauce to simmer for an hour so the meatballs are well cooked, and then leave to cool and put in the fridge for tomorrow if you're eating out. If not, I can come back and cook you some pasta to go with it." Her eyes find mine again. She's testing me, and Jasper has a shit eating grin on his face.

"Fine, we'll eat the shit you've made."

She picks the pan off the stove and begins to walk away; Jasper hesitates before grabbing her hips and holding her still.

She looks over her shoulder at him. "Let go, I don't want to subject him to eat shit. Blaydon will be more than happy to eat this *shit*."

I reach for the pan and take it from her awkwardly, trying not to burn my fingers. "Don't be a brat, Twink," I snap and she whirls around to me, slapping my chest.

"Fuck you, Sammy, you're the one being a brat. How pathetic are you? I cook for you and you're being a dick! You used to love my cooking!"

I look her over. "I used to love a lot of things. Shit changes, Twink, I'm not who I used to be."

Her eyes bore into mine. "Yeah, I guess running away really changed you, huh, Sammy?"

I step up to her, looking down at her beautiful face. Her green eyes never leave mine, and she doesn't back down from my large frame over hers. "Run away? Only those who have people to run from run away, River. That's what your daddy did, sweetheart. I had nothing to run away from."

Her gasp makes me flinch. I went too far. I reach for her but she pulls back. "I'm sorry, Twink. That was a shitty thing to say."

She laughs and tips her head to the side. "Don't worry about it, Sammy. You can't hurt me, I'm numb inside. Have been for four long fucking years, ever since the man I loved abandoned me."

Her eyes gloss over as she studies my face. "Is he really gone, Sammy?" she murmurs. I question her with my eyes, but she shakes her head as if pulling herself from a trance. "I'll be back in an hour to cook Jasper and Jase some pasta to go with the sauce." She picks up the box of cereal and pushes it into my chest. "You can have these."

She grins and strides out, both me and Jasper watch her ass sway as she does. "Fuck, you two have history, you sly dog! Why didn't you tell me that?"

I shake my head. "It never started, Jasp. There's nothing to tell." I open the fridge, putting the groceries away.

"Never started?" he scoffs. "It never finished would be more accurate, Sam."

I place my hands on the edge of the counter and let my head drop. "I thought I was over this shit, but just seeing her, she's become even more gorgeous. I just want to fuck her brains out to get her out my system." I exhale hard and push off the counter. "I have a piece of ass from school coming here tomorrow. I bumped into her at the store. She can help work River out."

Jasper laughs. "Only you could pick up a chick at the store on your first day back, Sam. And good luck working River out." He continues to laugh as he leaves me to my misery of knowing nothing will get me over her.

CHAPTER FOUR
River

Having Sammy act cold towards me hurt, but I also felt fire in my veins for the first time in years. Being around him brought back traits of the old me, the natural flirting and confidence Sammy always made me feel when we were kids, seeped from me as if we had stepped back in time. I wanted to slap him and kiss him all at once. I wanted to climb that tall, sexy frame of his and beg him to fuck me senseless, while pulling my hair hard. A shiver runs through me, making me close my eyes; I squeeze my thighs together and smile at the sensation of feeling turned on for the first time since he left. I want to feel real passion. I've dreamt of him, and woke up hot and sweaty, but seeing him in the flesh, God, I still love him. It hurt hearing him talk so flippantly about leaving us. I know he struggled when he saw Danny claim me, but he didn't even come to me to talk, to ask me why. He didn't fight for me, he didn't save me.

I enter the living room and see Blaydon sitting on the worn leather couch. He looked spaced out, his eyes are unfocused, his posture slouching.

"Hey, sis." He rises from the couch. "You always look happier when Danny's not here. Are you happy with him, Riv?"

I stop walking. He has never asked me if I'm happy with Danny, he just accepted that Danny and I bonded over our secret. Blaydon has no idea I'm only with Danny to protect him.

"Don't be silly, Blay."

I walk into the kitchen and pour myself a drink of water, and Blaydon appears in my view. "I know you and Sammy always had a thing for each other. He didn't know I knew, but fuck me, Riv, I'm not blind. I could see the way he looked at you, and you at him."

I gulp down the remaining water in my glass. "That was a long time ago."

He sighs. "I know, but I just don't want you to think you have to stay with Danny out of loyalty to what he did for us."

A tear escapes my eye. Four fucking years it's been, and only now does he say these things to me. It would break him if he knew what happened with Danny, and why I'm with him. I walk over to him and smile. I stroke his cheek and he leans into my hand. "I love you, brother of mine."

He nods his head. "I love you too, sister of mine."

A knock at the front door breaks our moment. "It's Maria, for me."

He frowns and I shake my head. "I thought you cut her loose?"

He shrugs. I roll my eyes and head to my room. I strip off my dancing outfit and slip on some jean shorts and a tank top. I shake my hair loose from the bun and pull my brush through it, leaving it hanging loose down my back. I leave my room to make food for Blay. When I enter the kitchen I find Maria rummaging through the cupboards.

"What are you looking for?" I snap, making her leap a foot in the air.

She clutches her chest and stares at me eyes bulging. "Holy shit, River! You scared the crap out of me."

"What are you doing?"

She looks at the cupboard and then at me. "Oh …erm, just looking for something to eat."

My eyes study her and she squares her shoulders. "Blaydon hasn't eaten. I was going to make him something," she mutters.

I snort at her. "You cook? Please. What are you really doing? Because if you're looking for things that belong to Danny, you won't find them in the kitchen cupboard."

Her face turns red, her lip curls in a sneer. "Then where, River? He didn't leave Blay enough!" I walk closer to her.

"He gave Blay enough for him. You need to supply your own."

Maria's breathing increases. "Whatever, River. This is bullshit! You think you're so fucking great just because you're in Danny's bed. Let's see if you're still smirking when I take your place!"

She barges past me and I let out a huge laugh. She is crazy. If only she *could* sway Danny into bed, she would be doing me a favour. If she only knew how much Danny despises her and how much he loves me. In some twisted, fucked up way, he really does love me. He feels like he needs me to live. He's so messed up from his upbringing, lost just like Blaydon, just like me. We're all lost and broken.

I make Blaydon a turkey sandwich and chips, pour him a glass of soda, and tap on his bedroom door. "Blay, I left you some food out here. I'll be back soon." I wait for him to shout "okay," then go next door to make pasta.

I climb the stairs to the porch and tap my knuckles to the door before opening and walking in. Jase and Sammy are sitting on the couch, eating a pizza from a takeout box. Sammy looks over the couch at me standing there with my hands on my hips, and chuckles.

"Mmm, yummy," he croons, shoving a huge bite of pizza into his mouth.

I walk into the kitchen and pour a glass of water before sauntering back into the living room and standing in front of Sammy. "You need a drink with that?" I ask, tipping the glass, letting the water pour all into his pizza.

I beam at him, proud of myself.

He jumps up, scooping me over his shoulder and running with me into the kitchen. I don't get a chance to react straight away, but when I see him go towards the back door, I scream and pound my tiny fists against his back. "Put me down, asshole," and he does. He opens the back door and throws me onto the grass where I land with a bump. I scowl at him as I lay sprawled out on the grass, my thighs slightly open. His eyes zone in between my legs. "You want me to get you wet, Twink?"

I gasp and bite down on my bottom lip, pushing my thighs together, trying to ease the throbbing between them. He looks me over and a knowing smirk lifts his lips. He bends down and before I can scamper away, he switches the hose on and points it at me. Freezing cold water blasts my body, and I gasp and splutter. Sammy laughs. "Mmm, I like you wet, Twink."

I can't help heating up from his innuendos, despite the freezing water causing me to shiver.

"Oh, God," he groans.

I follow his eyes down to my soaking wet, now see-through top, my nipples slightly tenting the material. I quickly put my hands over my breasts, and look back at Sammy to see him grinning from ear to ear, before turning his back on me to go back inside. I don't think about what I'm doing, I just rush him and leap onto his back. I shake my hair all over him and press my drenched body into his, soaking as much of him as possible. He stumbles forward a little, and then grabs my thighs that are firmly wrapped around his waist. I squeeze them and he grunts, "Loosen your grip, you'll crack my ribs!"

I laugh. "That's the plan," I whisper into his ear.

He reaches his arm around, grabbing at my waist and pulling me around so I'm straddling his front. He lunges forward with me pinned against his front and crushes me into the wall. I exhale all the air from my lungs as my back hits the concrete.

"Want to play dirty, Twink?"

"Isn't that the fun way to play?" I ask in a sultry voice, not recognising myself. Sammy bringing out confidence I thought had been lost years ago.

I'm flirting; Danny would literally kick my ass if he knew I'm wrapped around Sammy's waist right now. But he isn't here, and for the first time in four years, I feel free. Sammy's eyes search mine then drop to my lips, and then to my heaving chest. He closes his eyes, and when he re-opens them, they're cold. All the lust from before has gone. "You couldn't handle dirty, Twink. But you have always liked to play games."

I let my legs loosen and lower them to the ground. "That's such bullshit, Sammy. You have no fucking clue," I say, through clenched teeth.

I push against his chest, but he doesn't move, so I reach up again to add more force. He grabs my wrists and holds them above me, pinned to the wall. I squirm, trying to get him to release me, but he leans in so his hard body presses against me. "So clue me in, Twink, please. Clue me in because I never understood what happened." He breathes against my face, his breath heating my wet skin.

My body shakes with anger as I glare into his eyes. "Clue you in? Now, Sammy? Four fucking years later? You never understood because you bailed on us. You didn't care enough to come to me, to save me!" My voice cracks at the end, and I drop my head. His grip loosens and I use that to my advantage to twist free. I run.

CHAPTER FIVE
Sammy

Save her? What was she talking about? Save her from what? Fuck, I can still feel the warmth of her pussy against my stomach. I could have dry humped her against the wall, but instead my bitterness overtook me. What was she doing? She's with Danny now. I'm turning back into the needy fucker that left four years ago. I would have walked over hot coals for that girl. Save *her*? I was the one who needed saving after she tore my heart out and handed it to Danny to stamp on.

"Yo, Sammy, why did a soaking wet River just storm through here like a hurricane?" Jasper asks, poking his head out the back door and looking over at me, still standing in the same spot she left me in. "Does this mean no pasta? Because I passed on the pizza and now I'm starving."

I shake my head at him. "I can boil pasta. It's not rocket science."

Turns out it's not as easy as I thought. I'm supposed to use boiled water, not cold, and apparently I didn't leave it long enough when I eventually put it on the stove because it tastes like rubber. Jasper gives me the evil eye over the table for upsetting River and costing him a real meal made by her. I push my plate away and chug the rest of my beer to wash the pasta down.

"Well, look who learned to cook," my mother slurs.

She walks through the front door, leaving it open as she strides into the kitchen. She dips her finger in the sauce and smiles. "This is one of Twinkle Toes's huh? Didn't take her long to start molly coddling you again, Sammy." She shakes her head with a distasteful look plastered on her aged face. "That girl has the cheek to judge me!" She points her finger at my face. "She was crawling in and out of your bed since she was twelve years old, the little tart."

I stand from my chair, making it screech across the floor. "She needed comfort! You know what she went through with her mother killing herself."

She gives a bitter laugh. "Comfort. Is that what the kids call it these days?" She turns to Jasper, smirking.

"It was innocent, Mother. Get your mind out the gutter. Some people can be around each other without getting naked you know? Maybe you should try it!"

"Where's the fun in that Sammy?" She sniggers. "Is that why she jumped into Danny's bed? Weren't you up to it, Sammy? Women are just like men. Sex is comfort and your *comfort* clearly wasn't enough for her she needed to get it from your friend." Her dark laugh sent chills down my spine.

"You're such an evil bitch, do you know that?"

She hoots at me. "Calm down, Sammy. If it makes you feel any better, she's not happy. She's always sniffling in that back yard. God, her crying keeps me up some nights, she's a mess. No wonder Keith left them. Her and Blaydon are a right messed up pair. You kids always talk about us being better parents, but did you ever stop to think if you lot were better kids then maybe Janet wouldn't have killed herself, Keith would still be around, and I wouldn't need to drown you out with alcohol?"

My jaw drops to the floor. Did she really just say that shit to me? We're good kids considering we raised each other. She's making no fucking sense as usual. Jasper stands and walks over to her. "You know what, maybe you should have done what River's mom did because you are a waste of air, you spiteful, old, wrung out bitch."

She twists her face into a sneer. "Get out of my house," she spits at him, and he laughs.

"This isn't your house no more, bitch."

She shoves past him and staggers up the stairs. I wait for her door to slam, and then relax my tense shoulders. Jasper put her in her place while I'd stood frozen from her hateful mouth. I'm grateful to have him here.

We met in freshmen year of college and clicked straight away. We've roomed together ever since and become more like brothers then friends. Jasper's mom died when he was a baby, so he was raised by his father; a loving, stable parent, so Jasper didn't understand just how bad my mother can be.

I clear the dinner plates, then put Jase to bed. I slump down on the couch and grab the remote, flicking through channels. My thoughts go to River and what my mom said about her always crying. I felt my chest tighten when she said that. Was she miserable? Did she regret choosing Danny? Does she ever think *what if* like I do?

I open my eyes and realise I must have fallen asleep. My back is stiff, and some late night live poker crap is playing on the TV screen. Jasper must have already gone up to the spare room, the jackass, leaving me bent up on here asleep. I rub my hands over my face and stretch to my feet. I need water. My mouth feels like moths have flown in and set up camp. Leaving the tap to run so the water gets cold, I notice the light on in next door's yard, then River floats across the wooden platform, her body moving like flowing water, so natural and fluid. Fuck, I really am growing a vagina. She stops moving and clutches at her chest, dropping to her knees, a strangled cry ripping from her body, making my stomach twist into a painful knot. I shoot out the back door, hopping the five foot fence that separates our yards. I fall to my knees when I reach her and pull her into my lap. She gasps from the shock of me being there, then relaxes her body into me, gripping my shirt and climbing my body until her face is buried in my neck, her body shaking from her sobs.

"Shh, it's okay, baby. It's okay." My hand strokes her back, the other holds her head to my neck. When her body finally stills and her breathing evens out, I realise she's cried herself into exhaustion. I scoop my arm under her knees and cradle her back, rising gently to my feet. I carry her into her house and fumble my way through, opening the doors without disturbing her. When I reach her room, I don't recognise it. There's nothing left of the childhood bedroom I remember. The walls are now painted white, not the pale pink they used to be, and there are no posters. Her dance medals are nowhere on display, in fact, the room lacks any of River's personality. It's bereft; only a bed and a dresser with a chair in the corner fills the space. I lay her sleeping form down on the bed and look at her as she snuggles up to the pillow and sighs.

Damn, her face is all red and blotchy from her tears, but she's still the most beautiful girl I've ever seen. My eyes travel down her body like the fucking pervert I am, thinking about what's under those shorts she has on. She fell apart in my arms tonight and here I am perving on her tight, sexy little body while she sleeps. I'm acting like a pussy-starved teenager. I watch her body lift then relax with every breath, reminding me of all the times she curled herself into me when she would sneak over at night. I remember the first night she ever stayed with me; I'd heard her crying on the steps to her house. She rushed me when I walked up the garden path, coming home from a date I didn't want to be on, but River was too young for me back then, and Blaydon would never have understood my feelings. Her face was blotchy red, the same as tonight. When her small frame collided into mine, I instinctively wrapped her in my arms. "She's gone, Sammy she left us." Her voice was shaky and her body held a constant tremble.

"Who, Twinkle Toes?"

She released her hold on me so I lowered her to her feet. "Momma. She killed herself."

I felt her grief, I shared it with her, and took her inside and up to my room. I laid her down next to me and held her all night while she cried.

I blink back the memories, exhaling loudly, and rubbing my hands through my hair I reach for her lamp and turn the light off, close her door and leave.

CHAPTER SIX

Sammy consumed my dreams last night; I had once again found myself in a heap. Memories holding me hostage playing images of my sixteenth birthday over and over, overwhelming me, reducing me to sobbing in the back yard, but this time felt different; this time he had come to hold me. I broke. I'd waited four years for him to hold me again, and I poured my tears into him and prayed he would heal me. I dreamt it was him who came by that night four years ago, and not Danny.My phone vibrates, pulling me from the bed. I walk over to the dresser already knowing who the text is from. I know because he texts me at least ten times a day to tell me he loves me. I swipe my finger across my cell; Danny's name highlights the screen.

River, I miss you and love you, my beautiful girl.

My stomach rolls when I read his words. My dad used to call me beautiful, and it's my pet name from Danny, too. I hate hearing it. Danny loves me, but it's an obsessive, intense, terrifying love. Whenever he feels low, or threatened by any male attention I receive, he goes into a depression or a rage. Either mood results badly for me. When he gets into a rage, he tells me he would rather kill me than let me go, and with his tight grip wrapped firmly around my throat as he says these things, it's a threat I know one day he will probably carry out; erasing me from this world, leaving me as nothing more than a memory in time, in someone else's mind, an echo, a whisper, a ghost.

When he gets depressed, he showers me in affection. Unwanted affection. He's always so gentle when it comes to sex. He caresses me and whispers he loves me, and I tell him I love him back because he needs me to, but I never participate in the bedroom. I let him have my body, but he can't have my soul. My soul is broken, shattered into tiny pieces. Fragments of my former self that faded away when Sammy's face did, four years ago. My thoughts go back to Sammy. Seeing him yesterday I felt like he had brought some of the pieces of me home with him, igniting a flame inside a body that had been absent of any heat for a long time. I take a quick shower then slip into a pair of black skinny jeans, and my K's Motors work polo. I brush my teeth, scoop my hair up into a low braid, and grab the milk from the fridge. I noticed yesterday that Sammy had failed to pick any up. I knock on Blaydon's bedroom door to check he's up for work and I receive a grumble, "Yeah I'm up."

Smiling to myself, I cut across the lawn to find Sammy's front door unlocked. When I walk in, I find him sitting on the couch wearing nothing but a pair of boxer briefs. My step falters and my breath catches. My eyes rake over his muscular physique; soaking his almost-naked form into my memory. He's so beautiful my heart aches thinking of how he comforted me last night.

"Hey," I say, startling him.

He jumps up, holding a hand over his heart. "Fuck, Twink! You gave me heart attack! Do you know how early it is?"

He looks to his bare wrist and his brow twitches when he realises he isn't wearing a watch. I can't help but smile, and let my eyes molest his flesh. His boxers leave little to the imagination; they grip his hips just below that perfect sculpted V that men have when they've worked hard in the gym. His skin holds a bronzed tan, complementing his ripped physique. God, he's divine. His little brownish pink nipples stand to attention on his hard, tight pecs, his six-pack tensing with every breath he takes. I feel myself contract between my thighs.

He tips his head to the side and smirks at me, his messy, dark hair falling in his face. "Would you like me to turn around so you can ogle the full package?"

His voice penetrates my ears and blood roars through my veins. I've totally been caught. I could act dumb or…

"Actually," I say, then reach into my pocket to pull out my cell phone. I swipe the screen and hold it up in front of me. "That would be great, let me get the front first, though."

I click the camera and the flash sparks as I take his picture. His mouth drops open and his eyes bulge slightly. I bite my lip and then we both burst into a fit of laughter.

"What's so funny?"

My eyes reluctantly leave Sammy and glance up to a yawning Jasper, who is descending the stairs. He's also wearing only boxer shorts. His body is slimmer than Sammy's. Sammy is over six feet tall, and broad like a line-backer, whereas Jasper is slightly shorter and trim, but ridiculously ripped. My eyes scan him quickly before resting on his face. He is really good looking; dark hair, with light blue eyes, like Sammy. Damn, these two together must get so much action. "Twink was just taking pictures of me to masturbate to later."

My eyes snap to Sammy, a hot blush creeping over my skin.

"Is that right?" Jasper laughs and he holds his arms out. "Would you like a real man's pictures to fantasize about?" he strokes his hand down his stomach. "I'll even lose the boxers, give you the full works." He winks, and my cheeks feel like someone is holding a flame to them. Sammy's chest shakes with silent laughter in my peripheral vision. My mind berates me not to let them see me so flustered. I moisten my lips then narrow my eyes on Jasper's crotch and scrunch my nose. "Sorry, my camera doesn't have a zoom button."

I bite my lip to stop from laughing, but Sammy breaks into a loud stomach-holding belly laugh. Jasper's eyebrows rise nearly up to his hair line. He drops to the last step, grabs my hand and cups it to his crotch. "Mmm," Jasper says into my ear. "My package is plenty big enough to get you screaming, sweetheart."

He isn't wrong. His package begins to grow underneath my pinned hand and it's impressive. I know he is only being playful, but I'm not use to men being this familiar with me because Danny would kill them.

I gulp and look over to Sammy, who has stopped laughing, and now has a scowl on his face. Jasper laughs and releases me from his grip, walking into the kitchen. I cradle my hand to my chest like it's injured. I'm still rooted to the spot when Jasper strides back into the living room, holding a box of cereal and eating them dry, straight from the box.

"I brought milk." I hold the carton up and Jasper beams a perfect smile at me.

"Awesome."

"So, Twink, sexual groping aside, what did you come here for?" Sammy asks with a raised eyebrow and an annoyed edge to his tone.

"I thought Jase would need milk to go with the cereal," I answer, confused at his change in attitude.

"Well, you're a half hour late. My aunt picked him up early for a day at the zoo."

I check my watch. It's 7:45. "Oh, okay. Well, I'll just go, then."

I turn to leave, but Sammy's question stops me. "Twink, what's with the top?"

I look down at my work logo and then to Sammy. "I run the office at the garage."

He shakes his head, confused. "What about college? You were offered an early dance scholarship?"

My shoulders go limp and a sigh leaves my lips. "With everything that happened, I couldn't accept the scholarship. Blaydon needed me, and Danny..." I don't finish because saying Danny would rather kill me than let me leave him isn't something Sammy will understand. He grows stiff at the mention of Danny's name so I leave without a goodbye.

I leave feeling punctured. Telling Sammy I gave up the scholarship was so painful, bringing back the reality that I don't get to have the things I want. I belong to Danny, and I'll never belong to me or Sammy again. I walk down the path leading to my Mustang GT 500 that Blay had bought me when I was eighteen. Back then, it resembled scrap metal, but he restored it to its former beauty and I love her; she's my small sliver of freedom. I dig around my pocket and slip the keys out, unlocking the door and sliding in behind the wheel. The engine roars to life with a twist of the ignition and begins an aggressive purr. I'm just about to pull out when I notice an old Nissan pull up to the curb in front of me, and Chelsea Banks steps out. My stomach threatens to expel any remnants that line its depths. Chelsea fucking Banks. I hate that bitch. Memories of her with Sammy re-run in my mind like episodes of torture. Why is she here? I watch her apply more lipstick to her already overly made-up lips. I can't pull away, so I watch her saunter up the garden path and knock on the front door. Sammy answers, still in his boxer shorts. Her manicured hand rakes down his perfect abs, then with a smile from him, and his eyes flicking in my direction, he welcomes her in and closes the front door. I have no rights to him, but the squeeze in my chest hurts. Even after all these years, Sammy still owns my heart.

CHAPTER SEVEN
Sammy

I can't believe River had to give up her scholarship and is now running the fucking offices at K's. She's suffered so much since I left. Her haunted eyes hold secrets I'm scared of discovering. Why hadn't Blaydon got in contact with me? I was selfish to leave him. We were best friends, and it's only these last few months I even bothered to contact him.

I hear a V8 engine roar to life outside and I spring from the chair I'd planted my ass into to look out the window. "Fuck me," I mutter, looking at River sitting behind the wheel of a gorgeous red Mustang. I notice her watching an old Nissan pull up, and then Chelsea folds out from behind the wheel. There's no comparison. Chelsea is the definition of easy; her short, tight skirt shows too much, her make-up is plastered on, she's pouting and applying more crap to her face as she saunters up the path with River's eyes burning a hole into the back of her head. I smile and go to the door to greet her. Her eyes devour my near-naked body, an undeniable sexual glint in her eye. Her fake nails rake down my body. I flick my eyes to River and usher Chelsea inside. Once I close the door I point her in Jasper's direction. "This is Jasper, he's going to take care of your needs, Chels. I've got shit to do."

Jasper cocks an eyebrow, looking her up and down. She licks her lips.

"Follow me, sweetheart." Jasper smirks and leads her upstairs.

Chelsea had always been a slut. I remember when I first fucked her in the back of the cinema. We were on our first date; I was sixteen and hurting because Blaydon had told me River was going to a dance with a guy in her class. I wanted to be the one taking her to dances, but although our age gap is nothing now, back then it was a big gap. She was only fourteen, so I used Chelsea, and a couple of other easy cheerleaders, for a year until I couldn't stand touching them when River was the only girl who occupied my every thought. So I began the final wait. A full year of no dates, no hook-ups, just to be crushed at the end when River didn't wait for me.

I climb the stairs to my room, pull on some jeans and a t-shirt, and bolt back down the stairs so I don't have to listen to Chelsea wailing like a chick being cut up in a horror flick. I jog across the lawn and try the handle to Blay's house. It gives under my hand so I push it open.

"Yo, Blay?"

His head pops around the kitchen door. "What's up, dude?"

He's ironing. My brow furrows and he laughs. "You know my sis can't iron for shit, so that job's been delegated to me." He holds up a tiny K's work polo. "Not that this takes much ironing, but believe me, she still manages to come into work with wrinkles, so I iron her shit and she does everything else."

He grins, slipping the shirt onto a hanger. "What's up?" he asks, redirecting my focus back to the reason I came here.

"So, I know this is probably a delicate subject, but what happened with the garage when your dad left?"

His body stiffens. "We run it."

"We?"

He pulls his eyes from mine, picks up a bigger work shirt, and begins ironing it. "Me and River. I do the work and she runs the books and the office."

I cross my arms over my chest. "What happened with Saunders?"

"When Dad …was gone, we just took over. We did most of the work there anyway, man. You know he was hardly there. Danny sorted the accounts for me and it showed that Saunders was skimming off the top, pocketing himself extra cash."

Holy shit. Saunders was the manager of K's. He ran things because Keith was living more and more for the bottle.

"So, is the business in your name now?"

Blaydon pales and his hands shake. "No, it's still all in Dad's name. Danny got me passwords and account numbers for his bank and shit. We run it as if he never disappeared." He looks up at me. "Why?" His tone is cold, bitter.

"I was just curious. I saw Twink and I didn't know she worked there. I know she had a scholarship."

Pain crosses his face, his lips press tight, a gloss coats his eyes. "I love my sister more than life. She's the reason I breathe. I want her to have a good life, Sam. She's not the same person she was when you left. Neither of us are the same. Dark shit has plagued my fucking life, and as much as I tried to keep her in the light, the shadows pulled her in."

He's totally in his own world, his eyes gazing at the floor in front of him. His hand stills, the steam billowing from the iron now burns into the polo shirt. I reach forward, lifting his hand. "Oh shit, sorry. What was I saying?"

I pat his shoulder. "Nothing. It doesn't matter."

Shit has darkened River, but my girl is still in there. She's the girl who danced in the yard, she's the girl who sassed me when I challenged her, she's the girl who came over to cook for us and brought milk this morning. My girl is still in there, underneath the broken girl who now wears her face.

CHAPTER EIGHT
River

Danny has left numerous texts throughout the morning, telling me he'll phone me at two o'clock, and to have my phone ready. It's coming up to one o'clock so I put my cell out on the desk and debate ringing him to stop the stirring nerves in my stomach.

I remember the day Danny turned up with his stuff and just moved in to my house. He didn't ask, he just told Blaydon that he and I were in love, and he wanted to move in so he could be there for me when I had nightmares. Blaydon thought it was sweet. He was out of it most of the time, so he thought it was a good idea having Danny around for me. Little did he know, Danny was just there to tighten the leash he had wrapped around my neck the night of my sixteenth birthday.

I stare at the computer screen, rereading the order Stevie gave me to process three hours ago. My mind is stuck at the front door of Sammy's house. Where no-tits Chelsea Slut Face Banks had been this morning, touching him. God, I need to clear my thoughts. I need to get over Sammy. I can never be with him, Danny would never allow it, so why am I pining for him?

I press "purchase" on the checkout menu on the screen and drop my head down on the desk, banging it a few times while mumbling gibberish.

"That bad, huh?"

I look up, startled, to see Sammy and Jasper smiling back at me.

"Hey."

"Come on, we're taking you to lunch."

Sammy moves closer, poking his head though the glass partition and my breathing halts. He smiles, his eyes boring into mine. "Breathe for me, Twink, and get your bag."

I inhale, grab my bag and hurry out from the office towards them.

"Sweet place, Twink. This how you afford to drive that sweet ass ride of yours?" Jasper asks, looking out the window around the forecourt.

"You don't get to call her Twink," Sammy tells him and Jasper laughs.

"You don't own that nickname. I can call you Twink, right, Twink?" Jasper walks over to me and puts his arm over my shoulder.

I look to Sammy then back to Jasper. "Hmm, I'm not getting in the middle of you two."

Jasper bursts into laughter, and I squint my eyes at him. "That's a shame. We could really show you a good time if you were between us."

I glare at him and Sammy jabs him in the shoulder. "Knock it off, didn't you get your fill this morning?"

My stomach flips at that statement. Oh my god, Chelsea. They had a threesome. "That chick is crazy loud." Jasper puts a finger in his ear and wiggles. "I might need ear plugs if I go there again."

Sammy chuckles. "Can't be that bad if you're already considering going back there again."

"That chick is easy, Sam. Like *really* easy. She didn't even know me and she dropped those panties. I may call her if I don't find any fresh pussy while I'm here."

Sammy puts his finger under my chin to close my open mouth.

"Are you serious, Jasper?"

He looks at me, oblivious. "About what, babe?"

I flinch at his complete ignorance about the way he just spoke. I look up at Sammy who's watching me. "Is this what you're like too, Sammy? Did you leave us to live a life of *fresh pussy*?"

His eyes narrow and Jasper laughs. "Wow, hearing her say pussy turns me on. Is that wrong?" We both glare at him. "Shit, chill you two, I was joking. River, I'm sorry for being crass." He holds his hands up and gives me doe eyes.

"Well, look what the cat dragged in." A loud shout comes from behind us, and we all turn to see Stevie, his heavy boots carrying him down the hall towards us.

"Stevie! You still alive and kicking, then?" Sammy laughs, putting his hand out as Stevie gets close enough to grasp it. He pulls him into his chest and pats his back.

"How are you, son? Been a long time! You get the fancy college degree or what?" he asks in his deep, gravelly tone.

"Yeah, a business degree like I planned."

"So, have you come to relieve Twinkle Toes of her duties so she can wow the dancing world?" He grins and my heart misses a beat.

I watch as Sammy drops his eyes and shakes his head. "Plans change, Stevie." Stevie clicks his tongue. "Always thought you'd get married, you two. You were smitten with each other."

My eyes bulge and so do Sammy's.

Stevie laughs. "Don't look at me like that. I may be old but I'm not blind. You two were joined at the hip."

I cough to cover up the embarrassing meltdown I'm about to have. I feel the burning of tears in my eyes because Stevie is hitting too close to home. The thought of what might have been is agonizing.

"We were friends. She's with Danny now." Sammy laughs, but it sounds as awkward as I feel.

Stevie's face darkens. He hasn't liked Danny ever since Danny lost control of his temper at one of the mechanics for calling me gorgeous.

"Yeah, well maybe she shouldn't be," Stevie grumbles.

"So, lunch?"

Jasper cuts into the tense atmosphere and I could kiss him - after I bleach Chelsea off him, of course.

"Yes, let's." I smile.

"Did you put the parts order in, darling?" Stevie asks, as I push the glass door open and exit the building.

"Yes," I call over my shoulder before following Sammy and Jasper to the diner across the street.

We settle into a booth and Maggie, the waitress, comes over to give us menus. "Hey, sweetheart. Can I get you drinks?" She smiles, her red hair hanging loosely from her messy bun.

"Coffees all round, please," Sammy says.

I pick up my menu, knowing what I want but needing a distraction from Sammy's intense gaze.

"Burgers still good here, Twink?"

I lower my menu and nod.

"Here you go, do you know what you want to eat?" Maggie asks, placing cups in front of us and pouring the coffee. I notice Jasper's eyes glued shamelessly to my cleavage, and when Sammy follows his gaze, he tugs on his earlobe pulling his attention to him.

"They're not on the menu, Jasper! What's wrong with you?

Can you not be around women without being a pervert?"

I bite my lip to stop the giggle that wants to escape watching Jasper rub his ear and pouting like a child being scolded by a parent.

"I'm sorry. They're just there, staring at me."

I glower. "Well, they're not going to speak to you, Jasper, so keep your eyes up top."

"Oh, they're speaking to me alright!" He smirks, earning him a slap from Sammy and an exhausted sigh from Maggie.

"Do you want to order?" Maggie asks, tapping her pen against the pad she's holding.

"Burgers all round please, hold the fries on one of those."

My eyes find Sammy's; he's remembered I don't like fries with my burgers. Too many carbs makes me too lethargic to dance.

"So, Chelsea. Didn't take her long to get back on the scene."

Sammy's grin and the sparkle in his eyes tell me he knows I'm fishing. "I bumped into her at the store. She wanted to come over to catch up."

I grasp my coffee cup to stop myself from pounding the table. I gulp my drink, wincing from the burning sensation it leaves on my tongue.

"Hot," Sammy says, with a smirk.

"Hot? She's a slut, Sammy. Everyone's playing in that playground."

He chuckles. "You sound a little bitter there, Twink. I was actually referring to the coffee."

My cheeks flush, heat building all over my body. They both laugh at my embarrassment.

"You don't need to be bitter. There's plenty of me to share." Jasper grins, pointing down to his groin.

Maggie returns, placing our food down in front of us, and everyone digs in. Apart from groans of pleasure coming from Jasper, we eat in silence. Sammy pays the bill. He and Jasper walk me back to the garage.

"Come over for dinner tonight, Twink?"

I look between him and Jasper. "Is this your way of asking me to cook for you again?"

Sammy bit down on his lip and I swear I sway a little, my body losing the ability to stand. God, he's so gorgeous. My eyes fix on his plump, juicy lips; my tongue darts out to moisten my own.

His hand reaches out to stroke my cheek.

"Fuck, Twink you can't look at me like that."

His breathless voice fans across my face, my eyes flick up into his, and there it is. Glossed over eyes full of lust, clear blues dancing with need. My lungs stop functioning; I feel lightheaded staring into his blue eyes.

"Breathe for me, Twink," he whispers against my lips.

Jasper's cough breaks me from the spell that completely rendered me incapable of breathing. Sammy's hands leave me, and I mourn the loss with a sigh. He takes a couple of steps back.

"Okay, I'll cook," I manage to say before turning on my heel and hurrying inside. Linkin Park's 'Crawling' alerts me to Danny calling my cell. I race into the office, noticing the clock reads 2:35 p.m.

"Hey."

"I told you I was calling at two."

"I know, sorry. I went for lunch and left my phone."

His heavy breathing blasts into my ear.

"I was worried. I miss you. I hate being away, but I need to stay here a few more days."

The thrill of those words puts a huge smile on my face.

"Did you hear me, beautiful?"

"Yes."

"You're quiet. I'm sorry, I hate being away. You know I wouldn't stay away if it wasn't important."

"It's fine, Danny."

"Okay, well, I have a meeting I have to go to so I'll call you tonight my beautiful girl, okay?"

"Okay."

"Tell me you love me, River. I need to hear you say it."

I swallow the saliva filling my mouth and clench my fists, my nails leaving moon shape dents in my palm.

"I love you, Danny."

I feel the smile in his reply. "God, I love you too. Bye, beautiful."

"Bye."

A tear escapes my eye. I don't love him and pretending I do was easy before because I was numb. Now it feels excruciating to even say the words. The person I've always loved has come back, pushing the broken pieces back together, awakening my soul, making me feel again.

CHAPTER NINE
Sammy

I saw the need in River's eyes. It mirrored my own, and confused me to hell. She wanted me, I knew she did, but it wasn't just lust I saw in her green orbs. It fucking cripples me because I don't understand why she isn't with me. Maybe it's just built-up attraction, lust we need to sweat out.

"Dude, I thought you two were going to go at it in the forecourt earlier."

I frown over at Jasper, and he shrugs. "Seriously dude, you both need to work each other out. That much is clear."

I ponder his theory and snort. I could never work her out with sex, that girl was so much more than just her sex appeal.

"Oh God, your mom's back, and not alone."

I look over to the beat-up pickup truck and groan at my mother, pinned against it by some grey-haired old douchebag.

I pull over and jump out, pointing my finger in her direction. "Do you have to do that shit in the street?" I ask, glaring at the old dude.

He looks me up and down. "Who the hell are you?"

I fix him with a death glare. "I'm her fucking son."

He flinches from the hostility steaming from me. He looks down at my mother. "How old are you?"

I can't help the laugh that rips from my throat. The grey-haired old creep is put off by her having a grown up son?

"I was young when I had him," Mom spits, pushing him away so she can storm up the lawn to the house.

He looks flustered. "I'll call you," he shouts after her, and hurries to his truck. I watch him until his taillights fade from sight.

"Dude, your mom is Chelsea twenty years from now." He chuckles and I turn my glare on him before following her into the house.

"Mom, Jase will be home at five," I tell her as she rummages through the fridge, helping herself to my beer.

"I'm out tonight, Sammy. I only came back to grab some money. You can watch him."

I slam the fridge closed, snatching the bottle from her hand. "Well you can at least spend a little time with him before you go out."

She rolls her eyes. "Whatever, Sammy. I'm leaving now. I'll spend time with him when I get back." She barges my arm as she walks past.

"Fuck. That, right there, is why I never want a woman."

"You're not wrong," Jasper agrees, swiping the beer from my hand. "Let's play X-Box before your bro gets back and kicks my ass all night."

I follow him into the living room. "I was going to go over some of the information for next week." I grab the laptop from the coffee table.

"Come on, man. Let's enjoy this week before we get swamped with the workload of starting a business."

I tap the keys restlessly. "Do you think I should tell Blay our plans?"

Jasper's eyes search mine. "This was a dream of both of yours. Maybe with his dad out of the picture you could approach him with a proposal."

That was the plan all along, to buy his dad out and run the business with Blay, but now there's flags going up everywhere. Blay's drugs abuse, the fact his dad still owns everything in name, working with Twink, but not being with her.

"Listen, man, I'm with you whatever you want to do but you will need to talk to them. This is a rival business you plan to set up, Sam.

CHAPTER TEN
River

The rest of the day drags after getting back from lunch. I try to occupy myself with filing but my head just isn't here today. I log out of the computer and lock the office up. As I cross the forecourt towards the garage I see Blaydon under a car. Everyone else has already left.

"Hey, bro. I'm taking off. You need me to cook for you?"

"No, I'll grab something later."

"Don't work too late, Blay. See you at home."

I stop by the store on my way to get some ingredients to make pasta bake, since it's quick and easy to make. When I get to the counter, the checkout girl is gossiping with her friend, completely ignoring the fact that she has a customer waiting. I'm about to clear my throat to get her attention when she speaks.

"So, guess who came in here last night."

Her friend eyes light up, her lips tilt into a giddy smile. "Oh my God, erm wait, wait let me guess! Johnny Depp?"

"Johnny Depp wouldn't shop for himself! God, you're so stupid sometimes, Mel. It was Sammy Holder."

She literally squeals like a pig and claps her hands together. "No way. He's back?"

"Yes way, and according to Chelsea, he's back on the market."

My insides crawl. Was he ever off the market? Did he have a girlfriend before? Did he love her? Oh God, I feel sick.

"So, did anyone ever find out why he refused to date anyone his last year here?"

My heart pounds. I knew I hadn't seen him with anyone that year, but I assumed he'd kept it away from me out of courtesy. We'd had this silent agreement of looks and touches, ~~and~~ him constantly stating the amount of days until my sixteenth birthday, and that we would be together once I was old enough.

"Well, Mary told Jason who told Chelsea he was in love with a girl who couldn't be with him. It was some romantic tragedy." She sighs. "Anyway, he must be over it now because he invited Chelsea to his house."

And there's the final twist of the knife I'd felt in my stomach since walking up into their conversation.

"Ahem."

The checkout girl's head spins around towards me. Her name tag reads 'Ruby' and I know she's new because I've been shopping here for years and never saw her before.

"I didn't see you there. Do you need bags?"

I look at the shopping in my full basket and raise a questioning eyebrow. "How else would I carry it?"

She begins ringing up my items. I pay her and smile sweetly.

I pull up and go straight to Sammy's house. Jase's arms wrap around my waist as soon as I enter.

"Hey, buddy! How was the zoo?"

He frowns. "I'm too old for the zoo."

I run my fingers through his messy blonde hair. "No one's too old for the zoo, Jase."

"Hey, Twink." Jasper grins from the doorway of the kitchen. I walk towards him, Jase plastered to my side making me stumble a little.

"Hey Jasper, I just came to get dinner started. Where's Sammy?"

"I'm here, Twink."

I turn to see him carrying takeout bags. "Chinese okay?"

I lift the bag in my hand. "I thought I was cooking."

He tips his head up, gesturing towards the kitchen counter. I put the bag on the counter and Sammy does the same.

"Sorry, I thought it would save you cooking after working all day."

My heart beats a little faster as I look at his sincere face. "That's thoughtful, Sammy, thanks. I'm just going to grab a quick shower."

He looks at Jasper. "Dish this up, Jasp."

Sammy places his hand on the bottom of my back and guides me to the front door. "Is Blaydon home?"

I shake my head, not trusting my mouth to form words with him touching me.

"Well, I was hoping to sit down and talk to you both."

I turn to face him. "What about?"

Conflicting emotions play in his eyes.

"What about, Sammy? Is everything okay?" I place my hand on his arm, his skin hot to touch. My body pulses with need from the slight contact. God, we should have given into this years ago. He tenses under my hand.

"I plan to open up my own body shop, Twink. Like I always planned."

I pull my hand from him. "Here?"

He folds his arms over his chest. "Well, this is where I live, so yeah. Here." Heat flushes my cheeks as anger boils in my veins. The shop was Blay's life, the part of him that reminded me my brother still resided within him. He loved his job and Sammy opening a shop would risk taking all our business. "You can't."

He furrows his brow. "You know I always planned to have my own shop, this is what I worked my ass off for in college, to have my own body shop and I will."

My body reacts without my brain's permission. The slap to his cheek carries through the house, receiving a gasp from Jase and a cuss from Sammy. I bolt for the door, running across the lawn. I dig through my bag, desperate for the key. My fingers grasp the bundle of keys and I quickly unlock the door, and then I'm being pushed though it from behind. I stumble into the living room.

"What the fuck, Sammy?" I scream as he approaches me, stalking towards me like a predator. If this was Danny, I would quiver, knowing my life was about to end. But it's not Danny, it's Sammy and as he reaches me, forcing me backwards to the wall, I gasp, filling my lungs with the thick, lust-filled air in the room. He pins my hands above my head and forces his weight against me. "Breathe, Twink."

He smirks and I bring my knee up and connect with his groin. He drops my hands and staggers back, bending over in pain. I slip past him and run to my room, slamming the door, the foundations shaking from the impact. I jump when the door flies open. "Fuck. That was low," he growls.

"How can you do this to us, Sammy? Do I mean nothing to you? I thought we were friends?"

He lets out a humourless laugh. "Friends is to tame a word to describe us."

I glare at him. "You're acting like a scorned lover, Sammy."

He laughs louder and stalks towards me again. I back up until my ass hits the dresser. "We were never lovers, but we were a hell of a lot more than friends before you fucked me over. I should be the one asking if I ever meant anything to you!"

My heart thunders against my chest. "You know you did, but stuff happened."

"Yeah, I know something happened, Twink. You let Danny into your panties!"

"Fuck you!" I scream. The pain of his false statement cutting me like a physical assault. *I didn't let him, I didn't let him,* the young girl inside me begs me to scream aloud. Release the truth from the dark shadows that keep me shrouded in their dark lies and secrets.

He rushes me, and I slap him repeatedly. "I hate you, I hate you, I fucking hate you!" I chant, connecting my palm to his chest over and over, and then to his beautiful face. He grabs my shoulders and shakes me, and then his hand comes down on my cheek. It isn't painful, just shocking. Even when Danny's mad at me, he never strikes me. He prefers to show me how easy it would be to end me without the mess. He knows he could end me with just a hand to my throat, but his most torturous punishment is his softness. He is always gentle with me when he takes my body. He kills me slowly, with softness, and owns me with fear.

My eyes find Sammy's, his blue depths full of lust. Wet need pools between my thighs.

"You hit me," I breathe, my chest rising and falling with every intake of breath.

"Don't be dramatic, it wasn't hard, and you hit me first."

I lift my hand and slap him again. He purses his lips in frustration and then slaps me back. I inhale sharply, my eyes narrowing from the contact then pounce on him, ripping at his clothing.

CHAPTER ELEVEN
Sammy

River launches herself at me, tearing at my clothes. Her soft lips find mine and I groan. She clings to me like a monkey, her limbs wrapping around me tightly. She weighs fuck all; both my hands are free to roam as her thighs hold her around my waist with a firm grip. Her nails scrap over my skin so hard I know she's drawing blood. My little Twinkle Toes likes it rough, who would have thought? Her tongue probes at my lips; I open and massage my own to hers. She sucks at my tongue, forcing a moan from me. Her hands move up into my hair, tugging frantically at the strands. I back her up, swiping my arm across her dresser and knocking all her shit to the floor, lifting her ass onto the edge. I pull back from her lips to rip open the top of her shirt. The two buttons fly in all directions and the tops of her perfect round tits are displayed in a black lace bra. "Fuck," I groan, burying my face in her cleavage. I grasp the opening I made in her shirt and tear it straight down the middle, exposing her tits and gorgeous flat stomach. She's stunning. I reach for the materiel between her tits and pull, snapping the material in two. Her full, heavy breasts spill out as the torn bra falls to the sides of her body. Her hard, rosy nipples stand, straining into tight buds, begging for my mouth to devour them. I bring my mouth down to cover one nipple, my tongue tasting, swirling, and sucking.

"Oh God," she moans as my hands grasp her ass, squeezing tight. I raise my head and bring a hand to her hair. I tug her head back and bite down on her lip, pinching her nipple with my free hand, and she quivers.

"Yeah, you like it rough, Twink, don't you?" I say against her lips.

"Give it to me, Sammy. Fuck me," she begs, and my head swims with pure lust, building up need for this girl. I lift her under her arms and throw her onto her bed. I reach for her jeans, yanking them open and pulling them down her legs. Her heavy panting breaths are frantic, raising those amazing tits of hers up and down rapidly. My dick is so hard it's almost painful and I pop the buttons on my jeans to release some of the strain. My eyes devour the image of River stripped bare, down to her black lace panties. I devour every inch of her, submitting her curves into my brain to use every time I need a release. I've seen a lot of females naked, but none came close to River. She's pure fantasy perfection. Her skin soft to stroke but firm under my hand, her tits are full, with a natural beauty, not like those fake tits that stand to attention and don't move if she does. River's tits have a bounce when I throw her around; her waist is tiny but her hips are curved to womanly excellence; her toned dancer's legs are firm, defined. Her blonde hair fans out behind her. She looks like a goddess. I loosen my belt, pulling it free from my jeans, my eyes never leaving her body. She keeps bringing her legs together so I can't see the pink perfection between her thighs, so I grab one of her ankles, wrapping the belt around and tying it to the bottom corner bedpost. I run my fingers up from her ankle to her calf, dragging it slowly up the inside of her thigh. I feel the heat from her pussy the closer my hand gets to junction between her thighs; her wet need for pleasure coating her panties. I grasp at the lace brushing against her pussy and receive a cry in return. My lips turn up into a smirk.

"Mmm, you're fucking soaked," I tease and she whimpers.

I snap the lace in a quick tug, pulling the material away, and bringing it to my nose to inhale her intoxicating scent. "Delicious."

I reach and tug her other ankle, spreading her open across the bed. I use the panties to tie her ankle to the other post, leaving her beautiful pussy on display. I can't wait. I dive between her thighs, biting down, sucking, nibbling, and teasing her. Her hands tug my hair and position my head to where she wants my lips. I let out an amused chuckle, then devour her soaking wet pussy, lapping at her juices; her moans fill the room. I tease and flick my tongue above her clit, my tongue dancing around the soft pink flesh. When I feel her breathing increase, I suck her clit into my mouth and slip two fingers into her liquid heat. Fuck, she's tight. Her heated walls close in around my fingers. I crook my fingers to rub the front walls of her pussy, and she screams out my name, her body pulsing, her come rushing down to coat my fingers; it's the sexiest moment of my life. I growl as I pull away and whip my jeans down, surging forward and thrusting deep into her dripping pussy.

"Fuck!" I call out as her hot pussy welcomes my dick with warm, wet need. I thrust forward into her depths; my mouth finding her hard nipple.

"Oh, God! Fuck me, Sammy! Harder, harder please, Sammy!"

I have never been this turned on in my whole life. I can't get deep enough; I want to crawl into her skin. I pull out and back in, continuing to thrust inside her, hard, punishingly. The bed rocks and bangs against the wall.

"Oh, God, Sammy!" she moans.

Her hands rake the flesh on my back. I plant my knees on the mattress between her legs and pull her up against me, chest to chest. One hand around her waist, one on the nape of her neck, I impale her down onto me, getting deeper than I thought possible. I lean back, releasing one ankle then the other; she takes her freedom, placing her feet down on the bed beside my thighs and lifts herself up and down my shaft, continually impaling herself on to me. Our sweat-covered bodies, slick against each other, move with ease. I bury my face into her chest, sucking, nipping, and licking at her. She fucks me hard, her strength and stamina rival mine. She lifts her hips up so my tip is the only thing inside her, and she rotates her hips.

"Pull my fucking hair, Sammy," she cries out as she sinks back down with force causing us both to tense; her walls squeeze my dick, milking my release. Our moans mingle, her body collapses against mine. We stay like that, gasping for air. She wiggles her hips.

"Oh my God, you're still hard," she gasps.

I chuckle, lifting her from me. She crawls off the bed and stands staring at me, her cheeks flush pink, her hair all messed up in the best way. Her naked flesh glistens from our mixed sweat.

"I'm not done with you," I tell her.

She backs away so I hastily grab for her, spinning her and pushing her front against her dresser.

"Oh, God," she mutters in a breathless whimper.

Her chest lays flat on top of the dresser, my hand pinning her head, her ass prone in the air. I drop to my knees, my hand sliding from her head to her back. I use force to keep her pinned as I sink my teeth into her ass.

"Sammy, oh God!"

I slip my free hand between her legs, coating my fingers in our mixed juices, the moisture dampening her thighs. I run the wet finger up the crease of her ass, she gasps when I reach her tight little hole.

"Will you let me fuck you there, Twink?" I ask, breeching the muscle and stroking my finger inside her tight ass.

"Oh, God, yes!" she cries as I slip my finger out and stand. I grasp her hair, lifting her so her back is against my front. I bite down on her shoulder and cup one of her tits with my free hand.

"Get on your knees and use your mouth to lube me up. Get me wet so I can fuck that tight little ass of yours."

She spins around and drops to her knees, one of her petite hands wraps around the base of my cock; her eyes look up at me through her lashes as her mouth opens and her tongue darts out, tasting the tip. She bites her lip and moans, "You taste of me."

She sinks her mouth over my shaft. Fuck, her tongue puts pressure against my dick as her mouth coats me in saliva, sucking me deep.

"Fuck, Twink," I gasp.

Her free hand cups and massages my balls. I'm going to explode if she keeps this up. I yank her head back by her hair.

"Make it soaking wet, Twink."

She continues coating my dick in her spit, and I can't take anymore. I reach for her, bringing her to her feet and turning her so she's back over the dresser. I spread her ass cheeks.

"Hold on to the dresser. I'll go slow, but it might hurt at first."

As I breach her entrance, her hands reach back, digging her nails into my hips. "Fuck me Sammy, hard!"

She pulls me forward to thrust into her. I wince as I enter her ass fully, she cries out and I still. She's so fucking tight. I bring my hand round to her wet folds and circle her clit with my fingers. She relaxes instantly.

"Oh, God, please move. Fuck me please!"

I can't hold back, her pleas are driving me insane. She's as desperate for me as I am for her. I pull my hips back and then sink forward again and again.

"Yes, oh God! That's amazing," she moans. "You're amazing."

I growl, plunging in and out of her tight ass. I slip my fingers into her wet pussy, thrusting them up inside her; with every thrust of my hips I mimic the movement with my fingers. I tug her hair with my other hand and continue to rock my body into hers. I'm building fast, and so is she. Her inner walls contract all around me, her body convulsing with pleasure; her pussy floods my fingers. I pound her harder and harder until she's crying with pleasure. I give her everything I have, thundering against her over and over until my own need grows to an all-time high, tightening my balls. I pull my dick free and let my come shoot over her ass cheeks and up her spine. Fuck, it's sexy as hell seeing her skin covered in my seed. Her body goes limp against the dresser and I lean away from her so she doesn't have any of my weight on her.

"Oh my God, Sammy."

I smile, but the rattle of keys in the front door has her shooting up and spinning towards me.

"Shit," she whispers, her eyes wide with panic.

"Riv, you home?" Blaydon's voice reverberates against the door.

She rushes around me, opening the bathroom door and shoving me inside. She grabs a towel and wraps it around her body. I listen as she opens her bedroom door.

"Hey Blay, I'm just going to take a shower."

"Why you all are flushed? And your hair is all messed… you know what don't answer that. I'm going out tonight. I might not be back but I'll set my alarm for work."

"Okay."

The door clicks shut so I exit the bathroom, still naked. River's eyes drink me in, her bottom lip disappearing in to her mouth. My body vibrates with renewed energy. Fuck I want her again. I look round her room to stop myself from throwing her back down on the bed.

"Where are you in this room, Twink?"

Her bottom lip springs free from her teeth, red and puffy, begging me to suck on it. My eyes trace the beauty of her features up until I meet her eyes. There's an intensity that makes me feel so vulnerable.

"What do you mean?"

"I mean there's nothing in this room, no personality. Nothing that's you. Where's River?"

Her head drops then lifts, pain written all over her perfect face. "The me you're referring to, the River you remember, left here four years ago," she manages to say with no emotion in her voice. Her pain wipes from her features, her face stoic, void of everything.

Sorrow tears at my insides. "Fuck, River. I know your dad used to beat on Blaydon and that was hard on him but he loved you so much. I know it must be hard for you that he left."

Her eyes search mine, then a weird giggle escapes from her. "Yeah, he loved me." She shook her head. "That was the problem."

Her voice is cold, lost. She sounds so broken, my stomach churns.

"What does that mean, Twink?" I ask, scared of her answer.

Her eyes lift to find mine and my body tenses. I feel heavy, like lead has replaced my blood, and I'm frozen to the spot. "What does that mean, River?" I choke out, my voice shaking with fear.

My phone chirps, and the atmosphere that felt like a thick,

invisible thunder cloud disperses as her face relaxes and she smiles.

"I meant nothing. Answer your phone."

She walks to her dresser, pulling out a pair of dance leggings. My phone silences, then chirps again straight away. I bend over to my jeans and search the pockets, pulling my phone out and answering. "What?" I bark.

"Fucking hell, sorry, I just wondered where you are. You've been gone two hours. Jase went to bed and your mother just came home."

I hear a muffled sound down the line, then a whispered, "She's not alone, man."

I let out an exasperated sigh. "I'm coming now," I tell him, ending the call. River is now standing with her hair pulled back from her face, she's clutching a workout top and leggings tight against her impressive chest.

"I have to go."

She's nodding before I even finish the sentence. "Yeah, of course. I'm going to shower, then dance for a bit."

She spins on her heel, entering the bathroom and closing the door behind her. Dismissing me like we hadn't just devoured every inch of the other, after years of wanting each other. She gives me the best sex of my life and then acts as if I'm a one night stand she met in a bar. I swallow the unsettling feeling taking route in the pit of my stomach and throw my clothes on. I race over to my house. The front door is open and Jasper is yelling. He has some guy by the collar, pinned against the wall.

"What's going on?" I ask.

My mother is standing with her hands clasped, wringing them together like she's nervous.

"Jasp?"

"This douche gave her money and told her to suck his dick."

My eyes fly to my mother, then to the man Jasper has pinned.

"It's the right amount! I didn't know she already had someone here, I can wait!"

Jasper loosens his hold and turns to stare at me, confused. My hands are shaking. "What does he mean, Mom?" I ask, sounding more like a boy then the man I am. She shakes her head.

"Mom?" the guy asks. "Fucking hell, let me go, man!"

Jasper's hands fall away, and the guy rushes past me and out of the house.

"Don't look at me like that, Sammy. It's easy money and I enjoy it, so no harm, no foul."

She saunters past me and up the stairs. Stopping a few steps up, she leans forward towards Jasper, holding up the money. "Hey, he's already paid if you want to collect?"

He grimaces and backs away.

"Suit yourself."

I watch in horror as the woman who gave me life laughs at us. My fist collides with the wall, splitting my knuckles with a sharp sting.

"She has to go. I can't be around her anymore."

Jasper's hand rests on my shoulder. "Come on, man. Come have some food and a beer."

I bring my hand up to examine the damage, flex my hand and wince from the throb. "I need to shower first."

CHAPTER TWELVE
River

Sammy took me. He's been inside me, finally. He gave me what I needed; I craved him. My body ached for him, I didn't even realise until my body took over and attacked his. I'm a Sammy addict who was deprived for four years. I needed his touch, his scent, his voice. My body hummed with life after so long being dormant. The River who had left four years ago when Danny's face replaced the fantasy of Sammy's creeps back when I'm around him.

When Sammy left, every piece that was me, every part that was Sammy's River, left when he did. God, he thought I meant because my dad left. When he asked me what I meant about my dad's love being the problem, I nearly told him about my dad's 'love' for me. All the years he spent with me, he never asked any questions about my dad's over-touchy way with me. Or the fact that Blaydon took so many harsh beatings. It was normal for Blaydon to have bruises so Sammy never asked. How sad is that? He had so many of his own issues with a worthless mother, he was broken in his own way, just like us.

I slip in my headphones, scrolling the playlist until I find Bullet For My Valentine. I listen while the riffs and drum beats work their way to my limbs, pushing all the pain and broken parts of myself into movement.

My muscles burn. I keep pushing myself, stretching my limbs until they scream for mercy. The sweat dampens my skin in a warm mist, the heat emanating from my body layers around me like a fog. I'm just coming up from a walkover when I notice Sammy standing on the edge of the platform. I startle, stepping back from instinct.

"Hey," he mouths.

I pull the headphones loose. "Hey," I reply, short of breathe. I lean forward placing my hands on my knees.

"You've been out here for hours."

I look up at the bottle of cold water Sammy is holding out to me. I snatch it from him, breaking the seal and gulping big mouthfuls. The cold splash on the back of my throat feels amazing. "Thank you."

"I wanted to talk about earlier."

"There's nothing to say, Sammy."

There's no way I can tell him about my dad. He'll feel guilty, and then maybe question his disappearance. I can't risk that.

"Okay, fair enough. I agree, it was just something that built up and we needed to get out of our systems."

My insides go ice cold despite the heat pouring from my overworked body. He was talking about the sex, not my comment about my dad. Oh God.

I walk over to him, anger roaring in my veins. I drop my eyelids halfway and look up at him through my lashes "Is it, Sammy?"

His brow creases, his eyes searching mine. "Is it what?" His voice is hoarse. I smile devilishly. I feel so empowered, so full of lust.

"Is it out of your system now?" I breathe against his ear, before I bite down on his lobe. Our breathing is causing my chest to rub against his abs.

"Fuck, no," he growls, grasping my hair and spinning his body around mine so he's pushing his front against my back. He forces me forwards, pushing my exhausted, needy body flat against the back of the house. My cheek hits the cool panels first, my body follows. He uses his grasp on my hair to tilt my head back. "You'd better be wet and ready for me, Twink."

He releases my hair; his hands grasp the waistband of my leggings and he tugs hard, tearing them down my legs. I lift each foot so he can slip them from my body. His breath whispers against the back of my thighs, his teeth sinking into my ass cheek. I whimper from the sting of his bite, sending shockwaves of pain and pleasure through my body. He stands back up, his heavy frame pushing against mine. He kicks my legs apart using his knee and foot. He grabs my wrists in one hand and forces them up above my head; his grip tight, pinching the skin. I hear him unbuckling his belt and tugging his buttons open. He dips and then thrusts up into me.

"Oh God!"

The delicious burn, then fullness, has my heart pounding against my ribcage, my blood roaring in my ears. I relish the subtle pain as my body struggles to accept his full length. His free hand seeks my clit as he runs his fingers between my wet folds, thrusting in and out of me hard and fast. He needs to dip his knees to accommodate the height difference, giving him extra leverage when he propels himself upwards, nearly taking me off my feet. My cries of pleasure fill the still night air. Sammy brings his hand up from my sex and places it over my mouth; the scent of my arousal assaults my nose as the moist dampness coats my lips. It's so erotic to taste myself on him.

"You're so fucking loud, Twink," he growls, pulling himself from the depths of my sex. I push my ass backwards, forcing him to step back, and then rush to the back door, slipping inside. He's hot on my tail, reaching out for me and spinning me to face him. I bring my hand whirling round with me to connect with his cheek. His head whips to the side at the contact; the sting in my palm excites me. An angry, primal growl roars from his chest as he launches himself towards me, pushing me backwards. He grabs me under the arms and tosses me onto the kitchen table. The wood scrapes against my soft, fevered flesh. He forces my knees to part and stands between my thighs, pushing my shoulders back until I'm lying flat on my back, my ass balancing on the edge. He lifts my legs, laying them up the length of his torso, the balls of my feet resting on his pecs. His hot mouth traces wet kisses across the arch of my foot, down to my ankle. I reach up, clasping handfuls of his dark, wavy locks and yank him forward, his hard cock slipping back into my wet, welcoming depths. We groan in unison at the contact. He reaches forward, yanking down the small piece of material containing my breasts; they spill from my top. His thumbs stroke against my hard, sensitive buds. I feel my body heating all over, my mind and body spiralling into the bliss of Sammy's touch. I'm pulsing with pleasure, the air fills with electricity. My skin vibrates with every thrust he gives me. Sammy moves his hands to clamp down on my thighs holding me to him as he crashes into me over and over, the slapping of our skin growing louder with every deep thrust of his hips. My body slick with sweat doesn't stop the wood's friction burn clawing at my skin; I bend my knee and push my feet against his chest, forcing him from me. We both whimper from the loss of contact. I sit forward and push him back, his knees collide with a chair and his heavy frame collapses into the seat. I jump down from the table, turning my back to Sammy and sinking down onto him.

"Oh fuck, Riv," he moans as I take his full length into my body. The angle is almost painful and I love it. His thighs are open, his body leaning back on the seat, lazily. My thighs are pushed together between his, making my sex squeeze him tighter. I lift myself up and down onto him over and over, my torso leaning forward, my hands resting on his knees as I rotate my hips, savouring the feel of him inside me. When I only have his tip inside me, I tease him before forcing myself down hard and fast. I keep the same rhythm, and he gasps every time I push down on to him. His sexy noises turn me on so much, my sex tightens and pushes me over the edge.

"Sammy!" I cry out as my sex floods with my arousal.

"Fuck!" Sammy shouts, lifting me from him and bending me over the table. My hot flushed cheek meets the wood of the table, my nipples welcoming the harsh feel of the battered wood. He drops to his knees behind me and my body jolts forward from sensitivity as his tongue laps at my sex. His hands roam my body; I feel them everywhere while his tongue explores every part of my pink heated flesh. I feel myself building again, my walls tightening, an electric pulse surfs through my body, ending at my nipples.

"I'm coming, Sammy. Please, I need your cock!"

"Fucking hell, Twink, you're driving me crazy," he growls, grasping my hips and plunging himself inside me. I cry out while he shows me no mercy, thundering his hips against me; my own hips crashing into the wood of the table. I know I'll have bruises, but I need this, I need the forcefulness he's showing me. He wants me, but more importantly, I want him. I choose him to be inside me. He thrusts forward one last time before he goes rigid and moans my name as his hot come pours inside me. I can feel the pulsing of his cock and it's the best feeling in the world. He withdraws himself, our ragged breathing filling the silence. I wait for my body to stop shaking from the immense orgasms we just shared before I stand up and stride past Sammy into the living room. I feel his strong muscular arms close around me; his hot breath in my ear.

"Did I say I was finished with you?"

My body shivers. He lifts me off my feet and walks us towards the couch. He drops his grip on me and I land on my feet and turn my head to follow his gaze.

"Oh shit!" I screech, and jump behind Sammy's naked body. I peek around him to see Blaydon asleep on the couch.

"Is he breathing?" Sammy asks, pointing towards Blaydon.

"Yes, stupid, he's asleep! Quick, come on!"

I tiptoe towards my room.

"There's no use tiptoeing, Twink. If what we did in the kitchen didn't wake him, nothing will."

I shoot him a glare and hurry into my room. I go straight to the bathroom, turning the shower on and stepping under the cascading water. My skin is hyper aware of every drop that touches my sensitive, flushed skin. Sammy appears a couple of seconds later. His eyes are hooded as he appraises my naked form, and he swipes his tongue over his bottom lip. I feel it deep in my core.

"Are you sore?" he asks.

I nod slightly. "More of an ache, like I know you've been there," I tell him, my voice breathless.

His eyes close slowly at my admission. "River, I've fucked you so much and yet I still want more."

He steps towards me, pulling the glass door open and entering the shower with me. Our bodies are so close, they respond to each other like an invisible force, pulling us together.

Two hours passed while Sammy took me and explored every inch of my body with his mouth and hands, and then fucked me into a near coma in the shower. Now we're lying on the bathroom floor, naked.

"I'm dying," Sammy moans.

I giggle and it hurts the muscles in my stomach. "You'll live."

He turns to face me. "Your brother, Twink. How bad is it?"

My stomach rolls at the sudden change in conversation and pain grips my heart. I turn to look at a spot on the ceiling, and memories play like a movie in my mind.

"She's too old to be sitting on your lap, Keith," my mom's telling my dad. He glares at her and she leaves the room, leaves me there at his mercy. His hands come to my waist as he tickles me, making me squirm and wriggle on his lap. I feel him grow beneath me. I'm only eleven but I know what it is; I have an older brother, I've seen his porn magazine that he stole from the guys at Daddy's work, and I've heard his friends talking. I become as still as a statue.

"Hey Riv, bedtime," Blay says, coming into the room and taking my hand. He drags me from my dad's lap and takes me to his room.

"Blay, why am I in here?" I ask.

He smiles and throws some of my PJs at me. He seems so much older than his years. "Put them on, sis. Dad's been drinking again. I want you to stay here tonight, okay?"

I don't reply. I don't need to. I change and crawl into his bed and he turns the light out and lays himself down on his futon with a cover. The darkness consumes me.

I wake to my dad shouting, "You little shit! You won't keep me from my own daughter, you little punk ass!"

I hear the thud, thud, thud. Tears stream from my eyes. Light flashes, flooding the room, causing me to squint.

"Keith come to bed, baby." My mom's voice rings out into the room. My eyes come into focus and I see Blaydon on the floor, his covers tangled around his legs. There are bruised boot marks imprinted into the flesh of his back, as clear as if someone had tattooed them there.

"Twink? River? Baby?" I blink when Sammy snaps his fingers in front of my face.

"I'm sorry," I murmur. "My dad woke him one night by kicking the shit out of him." I sigh. "Even after Dad was gone, Blay had trouble sleeping, so he took sleeping pills and anxiety pills, became dependent on them."

I hear Sammy's hiss and I sit up and grab a towel to cover my body. His fingertips brush down my spine. "I'm sorry, Twink."

I stand and offer him a weak smile. "I have work tomorrow, well, actually today. It's really late, or early," I offer, lamely.

He chuckles while he gets to his feet, then strokes a finger down my cheek.

"Don't want me to cuddle you, beautiful?" My body goes rigid, then I feel myself shaking.

CHAPTER THIRTEEN
Sammy

She's gone stone still. Her beautiful, sexual flush has left her, a pale white taking its place. Her body trembles.

"Twink, what's wrong?"

Tears fill her green eyes, making them look like the ocean. She looks like she's in a daydream.

"Baby, talk to me, what's wrong?"

I stroke down her arms and this makes her tremble more. I'm starting to freak out, ~~so~~ I grasp the tops of her arms tight and shake her.

"River, for fuck's sake." I tap her cheek, not hard enough to hurt her, but enough to get her attention.

"Sammy?"

She's looking at me like she's surprised to see me.

"Twink, where did you go?"

She shakes her head. "I can't do that with you."

I step back. "What?"

She looks so lost and troubled, I just want to wrap her in my arms and shelter her from all the shit, but I know it's too late. The shit's happened and that's why she's like this.

"Cuddly soft stuff," she answers.

My body recoils. She doesn't want the cuddly love shit with me is what she means. She really does just want to fuck me out of her system. A dark laugh ripples through me. After all the girls I banged and discarded, I deserve this. Karma, she really is a bitch. I won't let River see how affected I am.

"Hey, that's fine. I'm happy to fuck then bail."

I turn and leave her standing there. I search the house for my discarded clothes, slipping into them as I make my way out the front door and across the lawn. My front door isn't locked as usual when I reach my house. I swing it open, fall onto the couch and let my heavy lids close.

"Sam."

I feel Jasper poking me with his foot. I groan and stretch out my stiff limbs. "Fuck off."

"It's noon, man. You've been crashed for hours, your brother wants feeding."

I look up to see Jasper and Jase standing there, dressed and looking at me expectantly. I rub my hands down my face.

"Okay, okay, we can go somewhere for lunch." I rise to a sitting position. "Where's Mom?"

"She left before Jase woke up."

I look to Jasper; he's shaking his head and holding a finger to his mouth. My brow furrows in confusion.

"Okay, let me change, buddy."

Jase grins and I stand and rub my hand over his messy blonde hair. I climb the stairs, pulling my shirt over my head and dumping it in the laundry basket on the landing. I walk into my room and stop dead at my reflection in the mirror. My body is covered in scratches and hickeys. I turn to see River's claw marks down my back, and a smile plays on my lips. I finally got to be with her, and she was more than any fantasy I ever had. Her body, her touch. Fuck, she was unreal and so animalistic. My dick twitches just thinking about her. But then she shrugged me off like I'm no one to her and that fucking hurts more than I can bear. It leaves a lonely feeling punctured straight through to my soul.

"Holy fucking shit," Jasper whispers as he closes my bedroom door behind him. "You look like you've been in fight with a tiger!"

I can't help the smile that spreads across my face.

"No wonder we couldn't wake you up this morning! Shit!"

I pull a shirt from the rack in my wardrobe and slip it over my head.

"So?" he asks.

I raise an eyebrow. "So what?"

He chuckles. "Don't leave me wondering, man! It's bad enough knowing I can't make a play for that hot body."

My heart begins to thud hard, and my fists clench. I hate hearing him talk about her like that. I want to throttle him. I exhale the aggression from my body. God, she has me in knots and about to kill my best friend for nothing. She doesn't give a shit about me. I let the Sammy that moved on and moved away take back over me, and I grin. "She likes it rough, and she's insatiable." I rub my hands through my hair. "I've never fucked that hard or come that much before."

He grins back at me and shakes his head. "You lucky fucker."

I feel sick talking about her like this. I love her. Fuck no, I don't!

"What was with the secretive shit downstairs about Mom?"

Jasper grimaces. "That's what I came up here for. She left, taking a duffle bag, and saying she isn't coming back."

I'm stunned. I never thought she would leave here, it's free fucking living for her. "Good riddance. Come on."

I nod towards the door.

Jase meets us at the bottom of the stairs with a grin. "Can we have tacos?"

"Sure, buddy."

I grab my wallet and phone, and notice I have missed texts. I scan through. When River's name comes up, I feel nervous, like a high school girl with a crush. I click it open.

Sammy, I didn't like how we left things. I think you misunderstood me just now. I just meant I don't want you to think I need the cuddle stuff. I like what we did. I understand that this sort of thing is normal for you but it isn't for me. You gave me something today, a gift that was taken from me a long time ago, so… thank you.

What does that even mean? I check the delivery time. Shit, she sent this last night after I left. I hit reply:

Twink, I don't understand what you're trying to say. Do you fancy tacos?

I hit send and throw my keys towards Jasper. "You can drive."

We load into the car and my phone chirps. Jasper gives me a knowing smile

"She going to let you heal before she tears you up again or what?"

I ignore him and open her reply.

SAMMY! Is that you asking me if I like women? Because I won't be indulging in the things you, Chelsea and Jasper got up to. No way!

I re-read the message with confusion and type:

WTF? I was asking if you want to have tacos for lunch with us?

A second later I receive her reply:

Oh my God! I thought you were being crude! Lunch sounds good. ☺

I slip the phone into my pocket "We need to swing by and pick River up."

We pull up on the forecourt and I'm surprised to see Blaydon working. He was so wasted last night, how does he manage to go to work like normal?

"Did I mention you're a lucky fucker?"

I follow Jasper's eyes to see River walking towards the car. She's wearing tight jeans and her work polo that stops above her belly button, showing off her tight, flat, tanned stomach. My jeans get tight around the groin area and I have to shift in my seat to hide the obvious arousal. Her blonde hair blows across her face from the slight breeze. She's pure fantasy. Every eye that's not Blaydon's watches her as she strides towards us. She grins and waves at Jase.

"Hey, I was wondering if I should take my car. I'm finished for today so it saves you having to drop me back here."

I shake my head. "Get in, Twink. Dropping you off isn't a problem."

She shrugs and slips in next to Jase.

"You must be starving," Jasper says, gaining him a death glare from me.

"Why?" she asks, innocently curious.

"Well, you never came back for your Chinese last night and I saw you dancing. That shit must burn calories, huh?"

If my eyes could set people on fire, Jasper would be charcoal right now. I look around and notice a blush creeping over her skin. She offers me a nervous smile.

"I definitely worked up an appetite, Jasper. It wasn't appeased with food, though." Her voice is small, but her words speak loud and clear. She knows he knows and she's letting him know she doesn't care. A shit eating grin spreads across my face and Jasper eyeballs her in the rear view mirror.

"I love you, woman. Marry me?" he tells her, making us all laugh except Jase who's looking at us like we're crazy.

"So, what did you think I meant when I said tacos?" I ask.

Jasper cocks an eyebrow as River blushes again. "Erm, well I thought you were asking if I like "taco" as in… a woman's parts."

My eyes almost pop from my skull. I look at Jasper and we both crack up laughing.

"I don't get it," Jase says, making me cough and compose myself.

"So who fancies going to the pier and riding the rides?" I ask.

"Cool!" Jase cheers.

We go to the pier and ride the rides. Jase insists River ride with him, so I get lumbered with a queasy Jasper who, despite our warning, insisted on eating chilli dogs for lunch instead of tacos with us. I'm fine with this arrangement as I get to sit behind River and listen to her laugh, and watch her face light up with amusement as the rides twist and spin us on questionable tracks. We have an easy, fun-filled day until Jasper starts retching and we're left standing outside a public bathroom while he empties his stomach inside the germ-filled hole. River insists I buy him some water from a vending machine outside, and let him lie in the back on the way home, his head on her legs while she strokes his hair like a mother would a child. He's moaning like a dying man when we finally got him home. River brings over some shit to settle his stomach and we put Jase to bed. We leave a sleeping Jasper, and go out to sit on the porch.

There's no breeze in the air, it's stifling hot. River has changed into a knee length summer dress; her bare, toned legs are driving me crazy.

"Remember when we used to sneak into the pool of the big house out back?" she asks.

I smile at her excitement and nod my head. Of course I remember, it was one of the best times in my life. River, Blaydon and I, sneaking in and messing around for hours, not worrying about what awaited us when we got home. She shuffles closer to me, her thigh brushing against mine.

"Well, the old man who owned the house died, and his nephew inherited the whole lot."

We never knew who owned the house that's just visible from our back windows. It's a huge mansion with a pool house. In the hot summer nights, it was a Godsend to sneak into to cool off.

"So how'd you find that out?" I ask. A little glint in her eye then a blush has me curious of her answer.

"His car broke down outside. I managed to use the car knowledge I've picked up from you and Blay over the years to get his car going again."

I'm impressed, and I bet he was too.

"Anyway, we got talking and I kind of mentioned that we used to use the pool."

I raise an eyebrow at her and she bites her lip, making my dick stir to life.

"He said I can use the pool anytime I want." Her voice has dropped in tone, her knees swaying, knocking against mine.

"He probably meant just you, Twink, not you and a guy."

I nudge her shoulder, and she drops her eyes to her lap. I dip my head to look up into her face. "But I'm all for sneaking in with you."

Her head shoots up, the carefree look on her face is so good to see. I jump to my feet, holding my hands out to her and she gladly takes them. I pull her up and drag her to my car.

"Will Jase be okay with dying Jasper?" she asks, as I push her head down and force her into the passenger seat. I fold myself into my seat and offer her a grin. "He's in bed anyway, he'll be fine."

I turn the ignition and pull away. I follow the winding road up to the mansion; it's dark out and the trees surrounding the estate offer enough cover to hide my car, so I park up and we continue on foot. I feel like I'm a teenager again, sneaking through the trees. I remember the last time we were here, River was fifteen, and Blaydon had brought Danny along with us. I caught Danny staring at River when she slipped out of her clothes. I couldn't blame him, she was wearing a red bikini, and even at fifteen, she filled the bikini out in all the right places. Her blonde hair sat over one shoulder, and I couldn't help sneaking up behind her and whispering, "Forty three days," into her ear. I was counting down the days to her birthday, and her little gasp had me leaping into the cool water to stop myself from exposing the effect she had on me.

We breach the clearing leading to the lawn. "Okay, so they have security lights now, so we need to sprint across and hide behind that tree," she whispers, and I laugh.

"Okay, on three. One, two, three!"

She breaks into a run and I follow close behind her. Light floods the lawn, making me pick up my pace. I reach out and pick River up with one hand around her waist. She screeches, then holds her hand over her own mouth to silence herself. I pin her to the tree, my breathing ragged. Her eyes are wide as she silently giggles, her body shaking against mine. Within a few seconds the lawn falls back into darkness.

"Okay, there are cameras up there," she points to the house, "but if we stick flat against the house they can't see us."

I raise an eyebrow. "You seem pretty confident."

She looks up at me. "Well I've never been caught. Let's go!"

I watch her sneak against the house, flattening her body against the exterior wall. She gestures for me to follow, which I do, amused at how young and carefree she seems. When we reach the pool house, River tries the door which opens easily and her face lights up. "Never locked."

I follow her inside. The outlay is exactly how I remember it. The rectangle pool dominates the centre of the room, and lounge chairs are positioned to border the pool. There's a shower room to the left. I watch River as she slips off her clothes, her eyes never leaving mine.

CHAPTER FOURTEEN
River

I watch Sammy watching me as I slip out of my clothes. His eyes devour me once I'm standing in front of him in just my underwear.

"You're stunning," he tells me, and I smile.

"Come get me, Sammy," I murmur, unhooking my bra and sliding it to the floor.

He steps towards me so I turn and dive into the water. The liquid swallows my body; the water is like ice and I immediately regret not checking the temperature. I surface, my whole body shuddering from the cold. My eyes find Sammy's, but he's not alone.

"Hello, River. Nice to see you again. When I said you're welcome to use the pool, this," he gestures around, "wasn't what I had in mind."

I swim to the edge of the pool where they're standing, both sets of eyes fixed on me.

"Mr Jefferson, I'm sorry," I stutter, the cold taking over me. He rushes to a shelf holding towels. He pulls one free opening it out, and handing it over to me. I pull myself up, fully aware that I'm only wearing black lace panties. Sammy grabs the towel and wraps it around me.

"Please, call me Derek. As I told you before, you're welcome to use the pool, I just assumed you would use the front door."

I scoot my body closer to Sammy, trying to use his body for heat. My eyes look at Derek nervously; he has a very commanding presence, an air of authority despite him only being in his late twenty's.

"We didn't want to disturb you," I say, lamely.

He smiles. "This must be Danny?" he asks, offering his hand to Sammy. Sammy's eyes narrow before he reaches and shakes the offered hand. "Actually, I'm Sam."

Derek's light brown eyes flash to me.

"Danny's out of town, Sammy's my neighbour," I tell him. I feel Sammy stiffen at my description of who he is to me. My face heats further at the thought of Derek knowing I was swimming topless with someone who isn't my boyfriend.

Derek nods his head. "Right, this must be a hard time of year for Danny," He says, thoughtfully.

My eyebrows pinch together and Derek notices my confusion. "I'm sorry. I'm inquisitive, it's part of my job. I tend to look into my neighbours and the people who sneak into my pool." He winks.

I'm still completely taken aback, and now nervous that he's been looking into us.

"I can see I've totally lost you. Come on River, you look freezing. That's why I came out here, to let you know the pool heater is broken."

I wrap the towel tighter to my body as I bend to scoop my clothes from the floor. "How did you know we were here?" I ask.

His eyes roam the length of my body then look upwards towards the ceiling. I follow his gaze. "There are cameras in here."

I flick my eyes to Sammy, who nods his head forward

gesturing for me to follow Derek. He leads us to the attached guesthouse and pulls out a set of keys, unlocking the door and gesturing for me to enter. He flips a light switch, bathing the room in light. The neutral colours give the room an airy feel, and Derek immediately leads me over to a fire place, turning it on. The plush carpet feels soft under my feet.

"Sit and get warm. You're freezing to death."

He rubs my bare arms, causing friction to heat my skin.

"Thanks."

I look to Sammy who is scowling at Derek. "So, Derek, care to elaborate on what you were saying about Danny?" Sammy asks, coming to stand behind me. Derek smiles down at me and takes a step away. "I just meant with it being the time of year in which his sister tragically died."

I gasp. "What?"

He raises his eyebrows then drops them his eyes apologetic. "I'm sorry, I thought you would know that. It's in public records. It came up on a Google search."

I lower myself into a leather armchair next to the fire place. "How? When?" I mutter.

He strides over to me, dropping to his knees in front of me. "I'm really sorry, River. It was ten years ago. She was eight and she drowned in the bath. Apparently, she was sick with flu all week and they assumed she passed out in the bathtub and slipped under the water."

I feel numb, how could I not know he had a sister, why wouldn't he of told me? Danny has never mentioned a sister to me. I look to Sammy. "Did you know he had a sister?"

He shakes his head. "No, he told me he's an only child."

"Why were you looking into us?" I ask.

He blushes, his eyes flicking to Sammy then back to me. He stands and slips his hands into his pockets. "I was intrigued when I met you."

Sammy's body tenses. "So, you're a stalker?"

"I'm an investigator," Derek says, his tone abrupt. "When I met River, I noticed bruises around her throat, and instincts took over."

I feel dizzy, and Sammy swings around fast to look at me. "What's he talking about?"

I stand. "I'm a dancer, I always have bruises," I tell him, defensively.

"On your throat?"

I shake my head. "Everywhere, Sammy. It's not a big deal." My look over to Derek. "I don't appreciate you checking up on us. If you had just asked."

I take my clothes and head towards a door, hoping it's a bedroom or bathroom.

There's a queen sized bed in front of me that I throw my clothes on, dropping the towel and hurrying to get dressed. I'm nervous that Derek has been checking into us and curious as to why Danny never mentioned a sister. There's a rap on the door, drawing me from muddled mind. I realise I'm fully dressed, and just standing in the room. I open the door to see a worried Sammy.

"Everything okay, Twink? You've been in here a while."

I shuffle out of the room not looking either of them in the eye.

"So, thanks for the deep freeze, but I need to get back."

I fake a smile and head towards the door. "You're welcome here anytime, River, and I'm sorry if I overstepped. In future, I will simply ask you anything I wish to know about you."

Sammy shifts and pushes me from the room.

CHAPTER FIFTEEN
Sammy

What a fucking creep that guy was. He was eyeing River with me standing right there. Pretending like he doesn't know I'm more than just her neighbour. *You are just her neighbour,* my mind mocks me. I have to break into a light jog to keep up with River.

"Where's the fire?"

Her small frame turns to me a with a weak-ass smile on her lips. I'm pissed that she's so upset Danny held something from her. She's been letting me inside her body and now she's pissed over her fucking boyfriend keeping shit from her. I fucking hate that she feels things for him, when it should be me. *It should have been me.*

"Nowhere, I just wanted to get out of there."

I shake my head and jump in front of her retreating form. "What's wrong Twink? Upset that lover boy didn't share that he had a sister? Maybe you're not as loved up as you think?"

Her face pales and she scowls at me and pushes my chest. "You have no idea what I think, and don't call him my lover, Sammy."

I laugh. "I'm sorry, I guess you're right. He's not lover boy, is he? I guess that's my title. Or am I just the neighbour?"

She narrows her eyes. "Why are you being an ass? You know you're more than just a neighbour. You're a friend."

I step into her space so we're nose to nose. "A friend?" I ask, my voice hoarse.

"Yeah, a friend."

I watch her chest rise and fall as her breathing picks up. Her eyes are half hooded. I reach for her, lifting her from the ground. Her legs instinctively wind around my waist and I back her up against the tree we hid behind earlier. I reach under her dress, gripping her damp panties and giving them a hard tug; they come away in my hand. She gasps and grips her thighs tighter. I stuff her panties in my pocket and tug the buttons open on my jeans.

"Just a friendly neighbour, Twink?" I breathe into her ear, before sucking her lobe into my mouth and biting down.

"A close friendly neighbour," she moans.

I pull back to watch her as I line my dick up to her slick, wet pussy and ram forward, impaling her onto me.

"Yeah, we are pretty fucking close," I growl as her tight pussy sheathes me. I retreat, and then plough forward again, her back slamming against the tree.

She moans in pleasure. "A good, close, friendly neighbour."

I continue filling her over and over again.

"A great, close, friendly neighbour," she calls out, and I take my thumb to her clit and add pressure there. My mouth devours the flesh on her neck.

"Oh, God, the best fucking friendly neighbour!" she cries, as her pussy floods, coating my dick in her come.

It was a hard, fast fuck, but I think I made my point that we're a lot more than just neighbours. She fucking owns me. She's always owned me.

CHAPTER SIXTEEN
River

I say goodnight to Sammy as we pull up at our houses, and rush from the car straight to my house. I hear Sammy calling me, but I don't answer. I lock the front door behind me. Blaydon is asleep on the couch; Maria curled up next to him. I run to my room and grab my phone from the bedside table. Danny has been trying to call. My stomach drops with nerves as I hit redial to call him back.

"River, where have you been? I've been calling you for hours!"

"I'm sorry, I got caught up in dancing and I didn't hear my phone."

I'm shaking; the phone is rattling in my hand.

"You need to quit fucking dancing if it's going to consume all your time. You know I worry, and you didn't even think to text me or call me? Do you even miss me?" I exhale, but don't answer fast enough for him. "Tell me you fucking love me, River, now!" I flinch and stare into the phone as he continues, "I know you've been out and not dancing. I called Blaydon and he told me you didn't come home today after work."

The tremble in my hand is making holding the phone impossible, so I put him on speaker and close my bedroom door.

"I was at the studio dancing, Danny, I swear. I have missed you."

He's panting down the phone. "You'd better not be lying to me, River. So help me God if I find out you've been living it up while I'm away working, trying to build a future for us. I will fucking kill us both! You belong to me in this life and the next, do you understand me?"

A cry breaks from my chest. I'm so conflicted, a part of me just wants an end to this façade. Can no one see I'm not here? I'm not breathing: I'm not living? I'm a puppet and Danny holds my strings. Most days no one resides inside me. I'm lost, my soul broken and weak drifting on memories of a time I was free.

"Tell me you love me, River. I fucking miss you so much, and the thought of what you're doing is making me crazy. I just love you so much, beautiful."

I full on sob. I'm so broken, how can I escape this nightmare?

"Don't cry, baby. I know it's because you're missing me. I love you, beautiful. I love you."

I suck in a breath. "I have to go shower now, Danny."

"Okay, then go get some sleep. I'll call you tomorrow, my beautiful girl."

I end the call and for the first time, I didn't tell him I loved him. I notice a text alert and my heartbeat crashes violently against my chest. I'm terrified it's Danny, threatening me for not saying the words back to him, but it's not, it's from Sammy.

You shot out of the car pretty quickly. Wtf? Can I come over?

I quickly reply:

Meet you out the back in ten minutes?

OK.

I take the quickest shower of my life, throw on some sweats and a tank top, and head out to the back of the house. Sammy is already there waiting for me, sitting on the wooden dance platform Blay built me. I walk to him and lower my body so I'm lying down, facing the sky. Sammy copies my pose, his hand reaching for mine, linking our fingers.

"Do you remember when we first met?" he asks.

A smile tilts my lips. "Of course. You were crying," I murmur.

He holds up a finger. "I was brooding, not crying. Guys don't cry."

"Broken guys do."

He stares at me for the longest time. "You know why I was upset?"

I shake my head, taking in the bright stars. "No, you didn't talk to me when I asked. You poked me in the eye through the fence."

"That's what boys do when they see the prettiest thing on this Earth. You're a girl, it's gross for a boy to think a girl is anything but cootie-ridden."

We both laugh, then his voice drops and I feel pain radiating from him. My soul hurts when he hurts. I stroke my finger over his as his hold tightens on my hand.

"My mother was hitting on your dad, while *my* dad brought boxes into the house. She showed no fucking shame, even when your mom came out to greet her. It was embarrassing for my dad. This was meant to be their fresh start from her cheating ways. We didn't even get the boxes in the house before she was back to acting like a whore."

I roll to face him. "I'm sorry you have her as a mother."

"I was born from a womb of a hateful whore. All I can do is make sure I protect Jase from her venom as much as possible. I wish he had a mother who loves him." He scrubs his hands down his face. "It's a hollow feeling, not being loved by anyone. I know my dad cared about me, but he didn't show me affection. He didn't show love."

"You were loved, Sammy. I wish you didn't feel hollow. I would have given anything to fill your emptiness with love."

His eyes hold a sheen. "Then why Danny? I don't understand what happened."

A tear escapes my eye. "I can't tell you, Sammy. It's so complicated and it's not just about me. I have to protect Blay."

His eyes question me and I understand why. I roll him on to his back and smash my lips to his. He doesn't move at first, but then his hands come up to my waist. He flips us so he's above me, and looks into my eyes before he slowly brings his lips back down to mine. His tongue slips out to stroke mine; I groan and tug his hair. He reaches for my hands and brings them above my head as he rains kisses down my face to my neck, but he's being too gentle and my heart rate begins to jump for the wrong reasons. I lift my head up and sink my teeth into his shoulder. He gasps, and looks up at me.

"Let me make love to you, River."

His hand slowly glides down and grasps behind my knee, lifting my leg to his waist. He grinds gently forward, his erection pushing against my sex. His lips trace my chin and neck, and a tear slips from my eyes.

"I can't do that with you, Sammy. It's what *he* does."

Pain and hurt pour from his eyes, then anger takes its place. "Fine then let's fuck!"

He sits up, rips down my sweats, unbuttons his jeans and plunges straight into me, hard. I scream out from the rough intrusion, but moan in the next breath.

"Yeah, you like it hard, Twink."

He plunges back and forth, sweat beading on his forehead. He flips our positions so I'm straddling his hips.

"Fucking ride my hard dick, River!"

He tears my top away from my skin, shedding it like an animal. His fingertips find my hard nipple; he pinches, making me scream in pleasure and pain. I lean forward to get better friction and raise my hips over him, fucking him with everything I have. My inner walls squeeze his length; I rake my hands down his torso leaving my mark on him. He upsurges, taking a nipple into his mouth, biting down and making me come all over his shaft. He tilts me back, grabbing my ankles and tilting me until I'm flush against the floor. He clutches my waist, lifting and pulling me on to him over and over until he explodes inside me, leaving us both panting. We lay there for a while, our laboured breaths the only sound filling the air. We're naked and still joined together.

"So you love him, then?"

His question throws me. "Who?"

He laughs and I feel his cock jerk inside me. "Who? Danny, that's who."

He slips from my body, pulling his jeans back on and buttoning them up. I feel the sorrow creep back into my veins.

"I have only ever loved one guy other than Blaydon, and he isn't Danny."

Confusion flashes in his beautiful eyes, and then he leans down, kisses my forehead and leaves me alone. I notice light streaming from the kitchen window and rush to pull myself together before Blaydon opens the back door.

"Hey, sis," he calls out.

I smile. "Hey. You okay?"

He shudders and scrubs his palms over his eyes. "I've run out of pills. Maria took my stash. She was gone when I woke up."

My fists clench. "How many times are you going to let her play you, Blay?"

He flinches from my verbal assault. "She helps me forget."

"I thought that's what the pills were for."

His sad, lost eyes plead with me to understand. "They're for sleeping. I can't fucking sleep in peace without them. He haunts me in the shadows, Riv."

He looks so young and fragile, and my heart bleeds for him. I want to scream into the night, I want to crawl inside him and pull out all the darkness that's taken him hostage. I know what he means about the shadows haunting him, because he haunts me there, too.

"Blay, come on. I'll lie with you."

I walk him to his room and lie next to him on the bed. He's sweating and shaking. I curl my body next to him, and he grasps my hand and holds it to his chest.

"I'm sorry, Blay. I'm so sorry for what you did for me."

His head snaps to me so fast I tilt mine back in reflex. "Don't you ever say that again. I would die for you, and kill anyone who hurt you. I'm your big brother, that's my job."

A tear leaks from my eye, soaking into his pillow. "Mom used to tell me that this life is a test. If we pass, we get to live in heaven, if we fail we keep being reborn to try again. Do you think she was reborn?" I whisper.

He turns to face me. "She failed this life for sure when she took her own life instead of protecting you."

I swipe the tear away. "She failed you way before she failed me, Blay."

I look at the scars scattered over his chest.

"Well, I'll never fail you. I'll always protect you," he says, and I know he would if he knew I needed saving.

"And I you. I love you, brother of mine."

He smiles. "I love you, sister of mine."

Sleep takes me. Dreams of our father beating Blay plague my mind. I wake with a whimper to an empty bed; the shower's running in Blay's bathroom. I gently tap on the door. "I'm going to make some breakfast, Blay. I'll leave it on the table for you."

He doesn't answer so I leave to get him some food. Without his pills he's going to struggle today. I need to phone Danny and find out when he'll be back.

CHAPTER SEVENTEEN
Sammy

She implied I'm the only other guy she loved, didn't she? I wasn't just reading into shit that wasn't there? Then why didn't she let me make love to her? God, my head is all over the place. Every ounce of feeling I ever had for her has crashed into me tenfold, and now I've tasted her and been inside her body, I can't be without her. I know Danny was there for her and Blay when her dad left and she felt she owed some sort of loyalty to him, but fuck, we owe it to each other to be together. We were always meant to be together.

I wake Jase up and pack his suitcase. We haven't heard from Sandra, the worst mother on the planet. I just hope Dad's new wife will show Jase some motherly affection.

"Hey, buddy. Fancy kicking the ball about for an hour before Dad gets here?"

He rubs the sleep from his eyes. "Okay."

I smile and place some clothes on the end of his bed, then go to wake Jasper.

"Yo, get the fuck up." His bare ass is hanging out the covers. "And put some clothes on. I've seen your ass way too much for someone who doesn't swing that way."

He chuckles. "Hey, I wouldn't blame you if you decided to swing that way after seeing my ass. It's pretty fan-fucking-tastic."

"As disturbing as that comment was, I don't know when my mother will show back up, so unless you want to wake up one morning with her on your dick, I'd wear underwear to bed."

He shoots up. "That's disturbing. I'll be wearing a fucking snowsuit to bed now."

I laugh as I leave him to get dressed. I come down the stairs and see River standing in the hallway. Her hair is pulled back, her tight top showcasing her amazing tits, her little waist begging me to wrap my arms around it.

"Hey." She smiles, looking up at me.

I inhale the smell of bacon from the plate she's holding. "Hey, beautiful."

Her body stiffens. "Don't call me that."

"Whatever." I snatch the plate from her hands. "This for us?"

She drops her eyes. "I'm sorry, Sammy. It's just… my dad used to call me that. It brings back memories."

Shit, I feel like a prick now. I stroke my thumb down her cheek, and when I reach her chin I raise her head. "I'm sorry. Thank you for bringing us breakfast."

She smiles. "I have to make sure you keep your energy up."

I half smile cockily "Oh yeah? You got some exhausting plans for me or something?"

She flushes a gorgeous red, and I have to hold onto the plate with an iron grip so I don't grab her and strip her naked right here in the hallway.

"River, you going to play?" Jase asks, bounding down the stairs and diverting my attention to safer things.

"Play?" she asks.

I take the plate to the kitchen, River and Jase following behind me. "Yeah. Jase goes home today, so we're going to kick a ball about for an hour."

Jase swipes a piece of the bacon from the plate and begins to chew on it like it's going to vanish out of sight if he doesn't get it down his throat quick enough.

River places her hand on his shoulder. "Sit down, Jase, there's plenty. Let me get you some juice. I can cook you some eggs, too, if you want."

He beams at her as Jasper walks in and slings his hand over her shoulder. "Have I asked you to marry me yet?"

She rolls her eyes and gestures to the empty seat at the table. "Sit and be quiet and I might make you some, too."

He grins and slides his now covered ass into the seat. "Yes, ma'am."

I pour us all coffee and sip from my cup while I watch River work around my kitchen, making breakfast. "So what's your plan for today?" I ask.

She smiles. It reminds me of when we were kids and she used to get excited over something. "I dance at the studio on Saturdays. I teach there now."

I can't help smiling back at her. I remember when she came to tell me scouts had watched one of her performances and were recruiting for a student to take a full scholarship at some fancy dance school, and they chose her.

"So, you're still at Bella's?" I ask.

"Yeah, she's retiring soon, though. She's hoping to sell the studio to someone who will keep it a studio. I don't know what I'd do if it wasn't there. It's been my outlet since I was five years old. It's a special place."

I watch the passion light her eyes when she's talking about it, and it makes my chest ache. I just want to hold her, love her, and be loved by her.

"You have two jobs, you must be rolling in cash. Why don't you buy it?" Jasper pipes in, reminding me we're not alone.

"I don't get paid for teaching. I teach under privileged kids in the area, to give them something to put their heart into. An outlet to escape the shit they were born into." She shrugs her shoulders and places a pan with scrambled eggs onto the table. "And I work at the lot for Blay. He keeps me and my car alive."

"You don't get a wage?" Jasper queries, astonished.

She shifts from foot to foot. "Erm, Danny says I don't need one. He buys whatever I need and Blay pays all the bills."

Jasper's eyes fall on me and I can tell by the perplexed look on his face he finds it as fucked up as I do. She looks at me from the corner of her eye, uncomfortable with the line of questioning. I turn to the back door.

"I'll get the ball. Meet you all at the front."

When I get to the front yard, all three of them are spread across both lawns. I kick the ball towards Jase and he passes it to River.

We've been kicking the ball for around an hour and we're all starting to suffer from the heat. Jasper gave up around ten minutes ago, and is spread like a starfish in the middle of the grass between mine and Twink's houses.

"I'm going to go get us all some drinks," I shout, pulling my shirt over my head and using it to wipe the sweat from my head. I hear Jasper moaning about the heat as I leave them for the cool shadows of my house.

CHAPTER EIGHTEEN
River

I watch Sammy slip his t-shirt over his head. Sweat glistens on his toned back, faint bruises from our steamy encounters mark his skin. My mouth was dry two seconds ago, but seeing him shirtless makes my mouth flood with saliva. He is perfection and I love him. God, I love him so much. I've never stopped and I never will. Feeling his touch was life-changing for me. He woke me up, pieced broken parts of me back together, healing a girl who thought she would never experience a wanted touch.

"Here," Jasper shouts, chucking his shirt at me. He gestures towards my chin and then his bare chest. "It's so you can mop up your drool. I knew you'd need it after seeing me shirtless." He grins and I throw his shirt back at him. Jase laughs and kicks the ball to my feet. Jasper wanders into their house so it's just me and Jase left kicking the ball around. He smiles at me and I feel the affection he has for me in his actions towards me. The doting glaze in his eyes when he smiles up at me. He really deserves better than what we all had to live with. I just hope his dad's new wife can give him some normality.

I hear a car pull up and my stomachs knots, fear and anxiety washes into me cleaning the happy feeling I had moments before straight from me. Danny steps out. He walks up to me and forces me into a painful embrace.

"I missed you. I came home early because you were so upset with me being gone."

He releases his death grip, and I weakly smile as his brown eyes bore into mine. They're so intense and dark, they remind me of the devil.

"Come inside, River. I need to feel you."

Sickness stirs in my stomach, and my hands tremble.

"I just have to finish up with Jase. I promised him I'd play until his dad gets here," I lie, hoping to buy time.

"Fuck him, River. He's nothing to do with you. Haven't you missed me?" He snarls and I swallow down the bile trying to work its way up my throat.

"Hey, Danny," Jasper calls, walking over to us, still shirtless.

Danny narrows his eyes at Jasper, then at me as Jasper hands me a bottle of water. "Here, River. Sammy's on the phone, he'll be out soon."

I'm ingrained solid to the spot. Jase kicks the ball towards me, but it lands at Danny's feet. Danny looks down at the ball then back at Jase. He launches the ball through the air with a targeted kick and it hits Jase full force in the face, knocking him backwards onto the grass. Blood explodes from his nose.

"What the fuck?" Jasper bellows.

Danny holds his hands up. "Accident, dude."

Jasper runs to Jase and Danny turns an evil glare to me. "Game's fucking over."

"Shit, I think you broke his nose!"

Danny looks over at Jasper. "You're being dramatic. Just because you look like a girl, doesn't mean you have to act like one."

Jasper scrunches up his face. "What did you say?" he asks, standing.

I dart around Danny and over to Jasper, putting my hand on

his arm, taking his attention away from Danny.

"Bring him inside, Jasper. Let me clean him up and make sure he's okay."

Sammy comes out with his phone in his hand. "Dad is going to be late." His eyes go to Jase bleeding on the ground. "What happened?"

"That asshole kicked the ball at his face," Jasper sneers.

Danny smiles darkly at him. "It was an accident, stop being a bitch about it."

My hands are shaking. I'm a nervous wreck. I don't want Jasper to rise to the taunting, giving Danny a reason to start a fight I knew he would win. Danny's tough, he endured years of violence like Blaydon, but instead of letting it defeat him, he found other people to let out his frustrations on until he was big enough to fight his dad back.

Jase's cries break me from my meltdown. "Bring him in, Sammy. I'll clean him up."

"No, Twink. I'll take him to the hospital. I think his nose is broken."

I look at Danny, begging him with my eyes to stop acting like such a jerk.

"Look, man, I'm sorry. It was an accident. Let me know if we can do anything."

Sammy studies his face for a few silent minutes before he nods his head and scoops Jase up in his arms. "Jasp, go get my keys and shut up the house."

I go to follow Sammy, but Danny's hand shoots out and grips my wrist. "In the house, now."

My eyes stay on the back of Sammy's retreating form.

"Now, River," Danny growls.

"You okay?" Jasper asks, looking at Danny's hold on me. Danny's grip tightens, making me wince.

"Twink?" Sammy asks, turning to me after closing the passenger door.

"I'm fine, just the blood made me nauseous. I'm going to wait here. Let us know everything's okay when you get back."

Sammy doesn't answer, just jumps in the car. Jasper follows, slipping into the back seat.

I know I'm in for hell from Danny. I pray Blay is awake so I can delay the punishment.

Danny pulls me through the front door and comes to a halt. Blay is sitting in the middle of the front room, rocking back and forth. I rip from Danny grasp and run to Blaydon, dropping to the floor and curling my body around his.

"Shh, Blay. What's wrong?" He's whimpering and muttering incoherently.

"Blaydon!" Danny shouts.

Blay's head snaps up and he gets to his feet. "You didn't leave me enough, Danny. I'm losing my fucking mind... he's here," he whispers, looking behind him.

Danny shakes his head. "I left you enough. Has that cunt been here, River?"

I know he means Maria and I don't know whether to be honest and piss Blay off, or lie and risk Danny catching me.

"She was here," Blay answers before I have to.

"I'm getting sick of this shit, Blay. I should leave you to fucking suffer."

Blaydon drops to his knees. "Just tell me where to get the supply and I'll get them for myself."

Danny laughs at him and I feel anger build inside me.

"You can't just buy them from anyone, they're prescription."

Blaydon's body is shaking so hard his teeth keep hitting together.

"Danny," I plead. "Please help him."

Danny's eyes pin me to the spot. "For you, River. I do this for you."

He pulls a bag from his pocket and throws it at Blaydon, then reaches for me and pulls me into our room. He throws me onto the bed and slips out of his clothes. I can't help the tears that escape from my eyes, my mind screaming. *Please, no! Don't taint what Sammy gave me! Don't touch me like that. I love Sammy. I'm Sammy's!* He reaches for my jean shorts and strips them from my body, then burrows his face into my sex and inhales. My whole body is screaming at me to not let this happen.

"I missed you so much. You belong to me. I'm the only man who will ever love this body, River. Do you understand?"

A silent sob puts pressure on my chest.

"I know that pretty-faced fucker wants what's mine, and you wanted to stay out there with him."

I begin shaking my head, but he grasps my face, covering my nose and mouth with his palm. "Don't fucking lie to me. I will bury that fuck before I let him near you. You belong to me, River. We're soul mates."

He enters me slowly. I cry and gasp for breath, but I can't get any air into my lungs. His palm is blocking both my airways. He's looking at my face as I struggle. I thrash my body as I panic, and he pumps into me.

"That's right, beautiful. Move your body. Love your man."

Oh my God, this is it. He's lost it, I've pushed him too far. Sammy's face floods my mind, his scent, his touch, his smile ....darkness.

My eyes sting and I feel exhausted as I struggle to open my eyes. The room comes into focus as I push myself into a sitting position. I'm naked, and Danny is sitting in the chair in the corner. He leans forward, placing his arms on his knees.

"Hey, beautiful. Welcome back. I'm sorry, we got a little carried away. You've been pretty out of it for a few hours. I must have worn you out."

He smiles and I try not to vomit all over myself. He is getting more and more delusional.

"I bought you something. I want to wait to give it to you, though. I need to sort a few more details out, but you're going to love it and we're going to be really happy, Riv. I promise."

He stands and walks over to me. He tucks some of my wild bed hair behind my ear. "I don't want you anywhere near Jasper, do you understand me?"

His grip tightens in my hair and I nod.

"Good. Go shower. I have to take care of something. Oh, and River, I don't like all the bruises from your dancing. You're covered in them."

I slowly stand, feeling weak and vulnerable. I put the water on the hottest temperature and scrub away Danny's intrusion. I'm just grateful he didn't realise all the bruises are from Sammy, not dancing.

CHAPTER NINETEEN
Sammy

I wave Jase off with my dad, glad he didn't go ape shit about the two black bruises that are forming under the kid's eyes. I'm pissed with Danny. Jasper doesn't like him, but I've known him a long time and I don't think he would have done something so shitty on purpose. I walk up the path and hear Danny talking, but it's not River who answers him. It's definitely a female, though. I open my gate and walk into our back yard; the voices are nearer now. I look through the hole in the fence I first saw River through, and sure enough, Danny is talking to some strung out looking girl.

"Maria, I supply Blay for his habit, not you, and you're starting to cost me."

She pushes herself against him, and he shoves her backwards.

"Let me pay you back, Danny. I don't know why you're with someone like River. I can give you what you need."

His face contorts in disgust. "Get on your knees, Maria."

She drops to her knees, smiling. I feel like a creeper watching them, but I can't believe Danny would go near her when he has River. There's no comparison. Danny opens his jeans. "Open your mouth."

She looks giddy, almost excited to get him in her mouth. She makes me sick, and my mother's face flashes through my mind.

He slips his tip in her mouth. "Taste. Tell me how it is."

She closes her mouth over his dick and I smile like a douche at the fact I'm bigger in that department than him.

"You taste divine, Danny. So good."

He laughs, pulling himself from her mouth. "Fucking right I taste divine. That's pure beauty you're tasting. Why the fuck would I go near your infested pussy when I have that to sink my dick into?"

She gags a few times, and my heart cracks and bleeds at my feet. "You let me suck your dick after you just fucked her?" she screeches.

He grabs a fistful of her hair and tilts her head back forcibly. "Now, listen to me. I'm sick of you trying to get on my dick. I didn't let you suck me, I let you taste her, because you're so fucking stupid to think you could ever compete for my affection."

She scowls at him. "She doesn't even want your affection, Danny. I'm not blind, I've been around enough to see she hates you."

He grips her throat. "I will fucking kill you. She loves me."

My heart is pounding. This chick's eyes are starting to bulge.

"Yo, Danny, is that you?" I shout over the fence. I hear shuffling, but I don't risk looking back through the hole in case he sees me and realises I've been watching him the whole time.

"Yeah, man. What's up?" I open the gate and see the chick scamper down the garden.

He steps from their garden and follows my eyes. "Blaydon's whore. I have no clue what he sees in the bitch," he says with a flick of his head.

I nod my head in agreement and change the subject. "So, Jase's nose isn't broken but he's going to be pretty bruised for a week or two."

Danny shakes his head. "I'm sorry, man."

I pat his shoulder. "Accident, right." I pose it so he doesn't know whether it's a statement or a question. "Where's River at? She'll want to know."

"She's showering. We had some catching up to do."

He smirks and it tears at me like a demonic beast ripping my flesh. The image in my head is one of the worst things I've ever experienced. I'm so fucked. I'm in so deep with her. I can't stand the ache in my veins.

"So Blay's chick seems like she would be a handful in the sack. Those types are dirty." I try bating him and he scoffs.

"They're cheap whores. I'd prefer my vanilla saint any day of the week."

I question him with a raised eyebrow. "Vanilla?"

"Yeah, you know. Make love type of girl. Missionary. Gentle, regular sex."

I'm shocked to hear him describe River that way.

His eyes narrow. "I shouldn't be sharing this shit with you, it's private."

I laugh and pat his shoulder. "Hey, guys can talk just as much as women about this shit, don't sweat it."

His eyes are still narrowed on me. "What are you thinking about?"

I laugh. "What?"

"You better not be imagining what I just told you."

Holy shit, he's deadly serious. If only he knew I didn't have to imagine anything where River is concerned.

"Hey."

We both turn to the voice that broke up the awkward talk we were having. My vision becomes filled with Derek-eye-fucking-investigator. What the fuck is he doing here?

"Derek, right?" I ask.

He smiles a knowing smile. "Yes. Samuel, was it?"

I laugh. He knows full well what my name is.

"I came to speak with River."

Danny reinforces his stance. "Who the fuck are you?"

Derek doesn't even blink at Danny's harsh reaction. "I'm Derek, I live near here. River helped me out when I was having car troubles. I just wanted to speak with her."

Danny steps forward. "Well you can't. She's not available now, or ever, so be grateful she helped you because she's a good person, no other reason."

Derek looks Danny up and down, then holds his hand out towards him in a friendly gesture. "You must be the boyfriend, Danny."

Danny relaxes slightly, but doesn't take his hand. "She mentioned me?"

"Of course. When I asked her to dinner she informed me her boyfriend wouldn't approve."

Danny's body is humming with violent intent, and inside I'm grinning. This Derek is playing him to get a reaction.

"So what the fuck are you doing here?" Danny seethed.

"I just wanted to tell her I'm leaving town for a few days. I've had the pool heater fixed, so she can feel free to come swim anytime." He turns his eyes to me. "And you too, of course, Sam."

Danny leaves without a goodbye and Derek chuckles. "Wow he's highly strung."

"Can I ask you a hypothetical question?" I ask him.

He looks serious when he nods, and opens his palms in a *go ahead* gesture.

"If I wanted help finding someone, is that something you do?"

He looks up at River's house. "Yes, but I warn you, some people don't want to be found and sometimes people are better not found."

I agree but I think River needs some kind of closure.

"Here's my card, Sam. Think it over and let me know what you decide."

I take his card and slip it into my jeans. "Thanks."

I go inside to find Jasper writing a shopping list and I snatch it from his hands.

Shopping:

Beer

Spirits

Snacks

I quirk an eyebrow. "Pretty short list."

He grins. "It's a party list. Thought we could throw that homecoming party tomorrow now the kid's left."

"Agreed." I throw my keys at him. "Go get some of the stuff now so there's not as much to do tomorrow, and I'll send out a mass text."

He jumps up, swiping my keys.

Thoughts of River rush into my mind. The things Danny said earlier about having sex with her left me feeling neglected and hurt. I risk sending her a text.

Hey, can I see you later?

I can't tonight. Tomorrow?

I'm having a party tomorrow. Danny said you and him caught up today. Is that true? Did you let him between your thighs with the ache still there from when I was there?

It's so much more complicated than that, Sammy. God, I wish it wasn't.

It fucking hurts to know you're in there with him while I sit here and ache for you. Do you even care about me? Do you love him, Twink?

Sammy, don't ever doubt how I feel about you. No, I don't love him. I've only ever loved one man. I have to go, I'll speak to you tomorrow, I promise.

My whole nervous system is on fire. I burn for her, and it's so fucking painful that she's not mine. I send out a mass text about the party, and then go to shower and lay my head down so I can stop thinking for a few minutes.

CHAPTER TWENTY
River

I wake feeling mentally exhausted after the texts with Sammy. I told Danny I wasn't feeling well so he let me sleep, but I tossed and turned all night, trying to think of a way out of my obligations to Danny without compromising Blaydon.

"I want you to stay away from Jasper at this party. I don't trust that fucker." Danny tells me as he comes from the bathroom, freshly showered.

"Okay."

He comes towards me. "I mean it, River. I will end him in front of everyone if he tries anything with you."

I exhale a frustrated breath. "He's harmless, Danny. Just because you see me as attractive, doesn't mean everyone does."

He laughs and grips my jaw. "You're so stupid if you believe that. You're the best looking girl any of those fucks will ever lay eyes on, and you're mine. I want you to wear your white dress. You look like an angel in that."

He smiles and strokes my face; I shiver from the touch, like death, leaving a chill in his wake. I throw on some clothes and make my way to the kitchen where Blaydon is eating cereal. "Hey."

I drop a kiss to his cheek and he stops me from walking away by pulling me into his lap, wrapping his arm around me and pinning me against him. His head drops into my neck and I wrap my arms around him and rub his back.

"You okay, Blay?"

"I'm sorry you had to see me like that yesterday, Riv."

I lean back so I can see his face. He looks so defeated.

"We only have each other, Blay. You see me at my worst, it's what we do. I love you, brother of mine."

He smiles, but it doesn't reach his eyes. "I love you too, sister of mine."

I stand, walking around the table to make coffee. "Sammy is having a party tonight."

"I know. Can I ask you something, Riv?"

I sit down opposite him. "Anything."

He pulls himself up from the slouched position he was in. "Would you ever leave Danny?"

My heart rate accelerates. "I couldn't. He might turn you in, Blay. I couldn't let that happen. Why are you even asking this?"

His head drops down. "River, he couldn't turn me in without turning himself in. He's an accessory. We would both face jail time."

I slump back, shocked.

"What are you two talking about?" Danny asks. He looks suspicious, his eye is twitching and there's a tick in his jaw he gets when his slightly nervous.

This can't be true. Would he really face jail, too? Oh, God. Could I have left him long ago?

"Just talking about the party tonight. You going?" Blay asks.

"Yeah, we'll be there. River, you mentioned you have to go to Bella's today because you missed it yesterday."

I nod. "Yeah, that's where I'm going after work. I just need to go in and order some parts for tomorrow morning. Shouldn't take long, then I'll be at Bella's for a few hours." I finish my coffee and leave them to it.

The day flies by. I text Sammy a couple of times, letting him know I need to speak to him about leaving Danny, and he's so enthusiastic, it gives me hope. Bella closed the studio early so I couldn't go there. She said she had an interested buyer going to see it, which made the empty feeling left from my childhood pay me a visit. If I don't have Bella's to escape to, I'll have nothing left that's me.

I arrive home late in the afternoon after driving around, trying to come up with a plan. I find Danny looking edgy, his shifting from foot to foot and it makes me edgy, too.

"Hey," I speak softly, trying to gauge his mood.

"Hey, beautiful."

"You okay?"

He smiles. "Now you're home I am. Get changed, beautiful."

I shower and change into the white sundress he left out on our bed.

"You look beautiful, as always. Blay's already gone over. You ready?"

I nod and smile.

The music is vibrating the walls, the hum of conversation blends in with the music. Red cups are in every hand. Danny pulls me through the crowd to the front room. I see Jasper, and he grins at me, looking me up and down in a slow, leering way. Danny solidifies when he sees Jasper blatantly checking me out, so I grasp his arm and turn him away. I watch Chelsea saunter up to Jasper and pull him off somewhere. I manage to move Danny further into the house, away from Jasper's direction, but he's shaking and gripping my arm so tight I know it will bruise.

"I'm going to end him," he seethes.

I shake my head. "I'm yours, Danny. I love you," I tell him, in the hope it will calm the rage inside him.

CHAPTER TWENTY-ONE
Sammy

Watching Danny with River is torture. Hearing him call River a vanilla saint last night was laughable; if only he could see the claw marks his *saint* left in my back, he might re-think that statement. River likes it rough. She's far from a saint and he is delusional. I walk up behind them. His grip on her arm is tight, and he's whispering something in her ear.

She shakes her head. "I'm yours, Danny. I love you," she tells him, crippling me where I stand. It's like someone has reached into my stomach and yanked my insides out. *'I've only ever loved one person,'* she told me. I'm the dumb fuck who believed she meant me. She's just looking for a bit of rough sex with me because the guy she loves won't give her what she needs. She's playing me again. God, why have I let her crawl back inside me, changing me, making me feel again?

I turn on my heel and go to the study; I need the bottle of Jack I keep in there with the wine, to keep it away from the greedy fucks at this party. I swing the door open and find Jasper and Chelsea; he has her bent over the armchair next to the bookshelves. Her knees are on the cushion, her hands holding the back of the chair, and he's on the floor behind her, lowering her panties.

Her smile grows when she notices me standing there.

"Have you come to play, Sam?" she coos.

I walk over and stand behind the chair, my crotch in perfect height with her head. I tip my hips forward and debate telling her to have at it.

I grab the bottle of Jack from the shelf as Chelsea eyes the buttons on my jeans; I unscrew the lid from the bottle, bringing it to my lips and taking a long pull. The liquid sliding down my throat leaves a trail of fire in its wake. I put the bottle back on the shelf and watch as Chelsea licks her lips, there's nothing from my dick not even a twitch.

Her body shivers with anticipation. Jasper grins over at me. He pulls a condom from his jeans and drops them to his thighs, exposing his already hard dick. The door swings open and River's voice floats through the room, her tone casual.

I turn my head, watch her walk in and come to a complete stop. Her mouth falls open and she drops the cup she was holding. Her eyes scan the scene in front of her; Chelsea bent over the chair, my dick in line with her mouth, her skirt up at her hips with Jasper below her, dick in hand. Chelsea tries to pull away, so I grip her hair to keep her there. River is so close, an inch more and our arms would brush against each other's. I pop open the buttons on my jeans.

"What going on, Sammy?" She frowns at me, tears brimming her eyes.

How fucking dare she act upset? I release Chelsea, reach out, and grab Rivers arm, tugging her forward so the front of her body collides with the side of mine. I reach up and grasp her hair in a firm grip. I force her head to mine, capturing her lips, kissing her roughly. She pushes against me, breaking her lips from mine with a shocked gasp.

I smirk and she brings her hand across my face, and fuck me, it stings.

"You asshole."

I push her against the wall, her small frame landing with a thump. I hear a flutter of activity behind me, then I see Chelsea rush out of the room with a "Call me," shouted over her shoulder. I have River's arms pinned above her head, my body pushing against hers.

"That hurt, River."

Her breathing accelerates. I tug her forward, forcing her body over the back of the chair Chelsea just vacated. She lets out a whimper from the impact, robbing her of breath. She's up on her tiptoes; her sexy little ass is now up in the air, presented perfectly for my access.

Jasper's still on the floor, dick in hand. I raise an eyebrow to him and he shrugs. I lift River's pretty white sundress above her hips and tear away her white cotton panties, laughing at the virginal appeal she gives off. What a joke!

"What would Danny think of his saint now?" I ask, bringing my open palm down across her perfect round ass cheek. She gasps and wiggles her ass, squirming like she wants to get free. I bring my hand down again, slapping against her creamy soft skin. She moans, her body giving her need away.

"Mmm, wait until I'm inside you before you wiggle. Jasper, give her something to hold on to."

He rises from the floor and kneels on the chair where her stomach lies against the back cushion, her hands trying to hold herself up. He helps her, bringing her arms up to rest on his shoulders, her body now suspended in the air, her head inches from his. She keeps her face tilted downwards, so I grab a fistful of her pretty blonde hair. She whimpers, then groans as I tug her hair sharply, and fuck me, it makes my dick twitch with need. I tip her head up so she's face to face with Jasper.

"No, Sammy. Not with Jasper here," she moans, totally

turned on.

"You don't want Jasper in here, but I have to share you with Danny? You get no foreplay, River. Punishment for you slapping me earlier."

She groans, her body is on fire. I can feel the heat from her pussy on my dick, and I'm not even inside her yet. I kick her feet further apart using my foot. Positioning my dick at her opening, I thrust forward, she cries out in pleasure and so do I. She is so fucking tight and hot inside her walls; her sweet, tight pussy coats my dick like a warm, wet glove. She takes my breath away; I have to still my movements to stop from blowing my load before I've started.

"Fuck," Jasper groans, his chest rising and falling. "She's gorgeous."

I pull myself out of her slick warmth and then plunge back in.

"Oh God, Sammy," she moans.

"Swallow her moans, Jasper!" I command, and he eagerly crushes his lips to hers, his hands gripping the sides of her head. He devours her mouth as I thrust hard inside her; punishingly penetrating her pussy with all the aggression I feel towards her for making me love her still after all these fucking years. My hand's still tight in her hair, tugging with every thrust forward, my free hand gripping her hip, my fingers digging into her soft flesh, holding on for dear life. The slapping sounds fill the air as I pound against her, turning me on more with every slap that rings out in the room. She's getting wetter and wetter, her juices flowing all over my dick; I'm delirious with need for her. I thrust harder and harder, in sync with her muffled moans. I pull her head up and away from Jasper's mouth so it rests against my chest. I have to bend more at the knees in this position, thrusting upwards. I lift one of her thighs to rest over the back of the chair to give me better access and tear at the front of her dress, yanking it down, snapping one of the straps in the process. Her tits spill out on display; Jasper hisses and River's body trembles with need of release. She tries to cover herself from Jasper's appreciative eyes. Jasper leans forward, gently tugging her hand away and takes one of her hard nipples into his mouth as my hand slips around the front of her to find her throbbing clit. I stroke her in firm, small circles as I thrust forward, grinding my hips with precise movements to hit her g-spot.

"Oh fuck yes, yes…I'm coming!" she cries out. I lightly pinch her clit in my fingers as she comes all over my dick; her walls tightening, squeezing me while her pussy gushes her come all down my shaft, wetting her thighs. I follow her over with a hard thrust forward, pumping my orgasm into her needy warm heat. It feels like the room is breathing with all of our laboured pants echoing around.

"Holy shit, her fucking moans made me come like a high schooler," Jasper pants, looking down at his come-covered abs. I release her hair and slide my dick from her throbbing core, causing her to whimper, her chest still rising and falling as she tries to gather her senses. She pulls her leg down from the chair and brushes down her dress. She looks down and screeches, "Oh my God, Jasper!"

I look over her shoulder to follow the gawks. There's a nasty purple bite mark above and below her nipple; teeth-marked bloody dents imprinted into her soft supple flesh. I glare at him.

"Shit, sorry. It was just so hot, and look at them they're incredible. I got carried away." He gives a nervous shrug, and looks up to River shyly. "Did it hurt?"

She's still inspecting his mark, then her head snaps up at the sound of his tone. "No, it wasn't your fault. Don't feel bad."

She rubs her hip, lifting her dress, then she spins and glares at me, cocking her hip out. A bruise is forming in the perfect shape of my hand around her hip. We were a little too rough with her, and I feel a flash of guilt. She looks panicked.

"Danny's going to kill me," she stutters, her body shaking from top to toe. She looks like someone has flipped a vibrate switch on her. Her eyes cast over with a lost look, and she brushes past me trying to fix her dress and bolts from the room.

"What was that, Sammy? I never thought you'd share her."

I never planned to, or ever wanted to, but my anger ruled my head and I ran with it. I feel sick and light headed.

"You okay, man? You look grey."

I wave a hand at him, telling him to leave me alone without having to say the words, and we've been like brothers so he knows I need some alone time. I reach in my pocket for my phone and hit River's name.

"Hello."

Her timid voice holds a hoarseness from tears

"Twink, hey listen. I'm sorry."

"Why, Sammy? I guess I knew you'd changed, but I don't think I can do things like that. I know you, Jasper and Chelsea did that but-"

I cut her off. "I never did that with them before, Twink. I was angry. I heard you telling Danny you loved him, and after everything, it hurt. You're consuming me and I can't seem to fight the way I feel about you."

"Why fight it?"

"Because you're taken, River, and I have to watch him with what I want so badly."

I exhale, defeated.

"I told you there might be a way, and you didn't give me a chance to explain. You just got angry and tried to punish me with Chelsea slut-face Banks."

She sniffles down the phone.

"Where are you? Where's Danny? The way you ran out saying he's going to kill you makes me feel like you're worried about him finding out. That doesn't sound like someone who wants to leave him."

"He had to go pick up some things for Blaydon, and I didn't mean it that way, Sammy. I meant in the literal sense. He *will* kill me if he sees these marks. How could you offer me up to Jasper like that?"

"I'm so sorry, Twink. I was caught up in the anger and I wasn't thinking. I hate that I let him see you like that. I let him have a piece of what's sacred to me. I'm a fucking mess, River, but I swear to God, I won't let Danny hurt you. Is that it, River? Is that why you're with him? Are you scared of him?"

Her breathing echoes through the line.

"It's so complicated. It goes back to my dad's shit. I have to go change before Danny sees me."

She ends the call. I need to give her some closure, and hope she opens up to me. I slip the card for Derek out of my wallet and send him a text asking if we can meet up. I leave the room to find Blaydon with that girl who was all over Danny glued to his side.

"Yo Blay, you got a minute?"

The chick eyes me up and down, making me feel dirty. She literally eye fucks me so I feel the need to shower.

"Yeah, man, of course."

I lead him back to the study. "You want something, stronger?" I ask, holding a bottle of Jack.

He grins and holds his cup out to me and I pour him double

shots worth. "So, I know this is a sore subject but I want some information about when your dad left."

His face pales. "Why?"

I swig straight from the bottle. "I think Riv needs closure. I know this investigator guy who can look for your dad."

Blaydon moves quickly, and I find myself pinned against the wall. "Get your fucking hands off me, Blay," I warn.

He leans in. "The last thing she needs is you trying to find him," he seethes.

"See, I don't think so."

He shoves against me, dropping his hold on me. I shrug my shirt back into place and glare at him.

"Did you ever wonder why I got beaten, Sammy?" he asks.

I flinch, the memories of bruises and marks that Blay always had assault my mind. "I know he was tough on you."

He laughs without humour. "Tough on me? Tough on your kid is making him earn money to buy his own shit. It's grounding them for stupid reasons. It's not punching them because they were standing in front of the TV, or kicking them to wake them up in the morning. Tough on you is not fractured ribs, and making you blackout from the beating they give you for trying to protect your sister."

My body goes on high alert. "What do you mean protect your sister?" I ask, fearing his answer.

He looks at me with sad eyes. "She loved you. You know, she changed so much that night. I watched as her light dimmed, I watched as her heart cracked."

I step closer. "What are you talking about?"

"I love my sister, Sammy. I would die for her. I would kill to keep her safe."

I look at him and step closer, reaching out and gripping his shoulders. "Blay?"

He shifts his feet. "My dad loved River in an unhealthy way."

My world tips on its axis, my legs give out and I crumple to the floor.

"My mom couldn't stand it; the way my dad looked at River. The way he would make her sit on his lap. He would tickle her and make her squirm. He would hold her a little too long, a little too tight, his hands roaming in un-fatherly places. I knew and so did our mother. Instead of protecting River, she killed herself to escape watching it. I took beating after beating keeping him away from her room."

I wanted to cry. I wanted to crawl into a ball and weep for my River.

Blay looks down at me and shakes his head. "I would kill anyone who tried to hurt her, Sammy."

He walks out of the room, leaving me completely head-fucked. Blaydon killed his father, that's what he was saying, and Danny must know, and that's why River is afraid to leave him. Tears sting my eyes.

"What are you doing on the floor?" Jasper asks, entering the room. I shake my head signalling I need a minute.

"Okay, well River is back out there, just so you know."

I stand up and rush past him. I get to the front room, and there she is in a blue sundress; her green eyes light up when they find me. I feel the ache gripping at my heart. Danny walks up to her, making her jump in surprise. He laughs and wraps his arms around her waist. Her sad smile imprints itself on my already battered heart. "Later," she mouths to me and I nod.

I turn to see Blay watching me watch her. I smile at him and he returns it, lifting his cup to his lips and downing the contents. He grabs his girl and whispers in Danny and River's ears before he leaves.

A couple of hours pass in a blur of dancing and drinking. I

go to take a leak and get shoved into the bathroom. I spin, fist raised, but see River standing there.

"Danny's drunk. I just took him home. He's sleeping it off."

I look around. "Shoving me in the bathroom was a bit dramatic, Twink. If you wanted me alone, you only had to ask."

I laugh before the conversation with Blay comes back to me, hitting me like a hammer. I reach forward and grasp her, pinning her to me. I squeeze her tiny frame. I stroke down her soft velvet hair. "I love you," I whisper and her gasp makes me smile. She pulls back and looks at me, tears glossing her stunning eyes.

"Come up to my room, Twink." She nods. "I'll go up first, okay?"

She sniffles and lets out a nervous giggle. "Okay."

CHAPTER TWENTY-TWO
River

He said he loves me. Not loved, *love*. He loves me. I felt the spark burn bright in my soul at his admission. I'd longed to hear that from him. I open the bathroom door and make my way up to his room. I open the door and slide in, closing and locking it behind me. He's lying on his bed; it's the same from when we were kids. I smile at the nostalgia that cloaks this room. He pats the bed, so I walk over and sit down next to him.

"I want us to be together, Twink. I love you."

I lean down and kiss his lips. He pulls me down and covers my body with his. The way he's looking at me sends electricity racing through my body. I'm on fire for him. He gently plants kisses down my face and across my neck. He gathers my dress at the hem and coaxes me to lift slightly so he can take it from my body, leaving my breasts bare. My cotton panties are the only thing left on me.

"You're stunning, River. I love you."

He nips at my full breasts and I whimper in his hold.

"I can't do soft with you," I moan.

His hand drops to my panties. He rubs over my wet sex, his mouth devouring me as his kisses drop to my stomach, his tongue dipping into my belly button and swirling before continuing its journey south. His teeth pick up my panties and he drags them down my legs. I'm panting with need as he lifts my leg and begins trailing his kisses upwards. When he reaches my sex, he swipes his tongue out, making me call out his name.

"You're breath-taking, so precious, Twink."

His lips close around my clit and I feel the dull ache build in my stomach. His mouth and tongue worship me, making me squirm and quiver. I feel his finger breach my opening so I open my legs further, welcoming him inside. I didn't think I could handle soft with Sammy, because Danny was always so gentle. But Sammy's worship is so breathtakingly beautiful, It feels completely different to any feeling or emotion I've ever experienced, or knew possible. I feel him curl his finger, finding my g-spot and detonating an explosive orgasm.

"Sammy, Sammy, oh God, yes!" I scream out. He rides out the wave with me until my legs stop trembling. He kisses down my other leg, and when he gets to my ankle, he encourages me to turn onto my stomach; his kisses then begin their journey up the back of my leg. He swirls his tongue across the back of my knee, sending little jolts of pleasure up into my sex; his hands groping the globes of my ass. His teeth sink into my flesh when his mouth reaches my ass and I call out again. I feel his hands everywhere, his mouth travels up my spine and I feel treasured, loved. He gathers my hair and pulls it to the side so he can kiss my neck.

"I love you," he whispers as he enters me from behind. "God, Twink you're so warm and tight. Let me in, baby."

I lift my ass and bring my knees up, presenting myself to him. He leans back, grasping my hips and pushing deep into me. With a moan, he drives himself in and out of my warm heat. Sweat beads down my spine and I move my hips, gyrating against him.

"Pull my hair, Sammy," I beg.

He groans, wrapping his arms around my waist and lifting my body so my back's flush against his chest. I feel his hard cock thrusting deeper and deeper with every drive forward. He turns my face with one hand so he can caress my lips with his while his other hand massages my breasts. We're panting, our bodies ablaze with passion; he twists his hip and I fall apart around him; tingles shoot through my body as I pulse around him, igniting his own release. We collapse forward onto his bed, breathing heavily.

"Thank you," he murmurs.

I look over at him. "What for?"

He smiles and strokes my sweaty brow. "For letting me love you."

My heart pounds. "Sammy. I lo…"

Pounding at the door cuts me off before I can tell him.

"Sammy, Danny's back looking for River," we hear Jasper shout through the door.

My body goes taut, bile rising up my throat.

"River, get dressed. I'll go stall him."

Sammy throws his clothes on and hops out of the room, trying to get his shoe on. I rush to get back in my dress and run to his dresser, trying to tame my hair in his mirror. My cheeks look flushed from my orgasm. I run to his window, opening it and praying the air cools my cheeks. I give it a short while, then take my chances. Leaving Sammy's room I find Danny a few minutes later in the hallway. He looks mad, his jaw tight, that fiery gaze locks onto me. He grips my wrist. "Why did you come back here without me?"

I smile. "I'm going to help tidy up. I didn't want to listen to Blay and that slut going at it at our place."

He grimaces then relaxes. "I need to go somewhere. Will you be okay?"

I don't ask him where he has to go at one o'clock in the

morning while he's intoxicated, I just nod. "Of course."

He looks at the few people lingering around then kisses me full on the lips, his tongue forcing its way into my mouth.

He pulls back. "I love you. Be back when I can, okay?"

I nod again and watch him leave. Once his retreating form disappears into the night, I let out the breath I was holding; I turn to see the pained blue depths of Sammy's eyes. I follow him as he pushes his way to the back yard.

"Sammy!" I call out.

Once we're alone, he turns and rushes towards me, his hand swiping across my mouth to wipe Danny's kiss away. "I know why you're with him."

My heart begins in drumming against my ribcage flashes of my past echoing in my mind.

"Blaydon told me the kind of love your dad had for you, River. That's not love, and neither is guilting you into being with someone just because he knows your secrets. I love you. I love everything that you are."

I stumble backwards, shaking. My mouth opens and the scared girl's voice tumbles out. "Do you love all of me, Sammy? Because this," I point down at myself, "this is a lie. This is the lie I show to you and Blaydon; the lie I wear every day for you and for everyone so you won't have to see the damaged, broken girl underneath. This smile, these clothes, they're not me. I'm tainted, Sammy. I'm shattered. My mother took some of me with her when she died, my dad took some when he made me sit on his lap while he violated me, and more when he beat Blaydon for stopping him from raping me, and then you left, taking the rest of me, leaving my soul bare and exposed for Danny to capture and hold hostage. Can you fix me, Sammy? Can you want something so ruined and destroyed? Can you put me back together and make me whole again? Because whatever is left of me, the real me, you have her. You own all of her, all that's left. My thoughts, my body, and my heart. Can you save me? Sammy, please save me. Please save me."

I collapse to the ground and sob. Sammy bundles me into his lap and strokes my back. "Shh, don't cry. I love you, and I'll try every God damn day to save you, River, I promise. I'll save you, baby."

I grip onto him like he might vanish if I didn't hold on tight. I soak all those years of pain into his shoulder, silently begging him to take them from me and make me whole again. We sat there for hours until Jasper came out and broke our moment.

"Yo, someone threw up in the washing machine. What is *wrong* with people? The fucking washing machine, man."

I let out a giggle and feel Sammy's body shaking with his own laughter.

"I should help get things tidied," I murmur.

"No way are you clearing up someone's puke. Go home, take a shower and try to get some sleep. We're going to sit down and make a plan tomorrow."

His lips come down to mine in a gentle stroke. "I love you," he whispers.

I smile. "I love you, too," I murmur back. His huge grin makes the wait worth it.

I walk into my room and flip the light switch. Danny isn't back yet so I turn on the shower and let the day wash from my body; thoughts of Sammy bring a smile to my face. I step out of the shower and wrap a towel around my body then slip into the bedroom, and startle when I see Danny standing in the doorway.

"Sorry, beautiful. Did I scare you?"

I giggle nervously and grip the towel tighter around myself. If he removes it, he'll see the marks Jasper and Sammy left.

"Come here, beautiful. I need to feel your love."

Oh God. He will kill me.

"Can I just put some clothes on? It's that time of the month. I just noticed in the shower. That's why I didn't feel well yesterday," I lie, praying he doesn't catch me in it.

He walks over to me and strokes his hands down my arms. "Okay, go get dressed. I'll get you a hot water bottle."

I pull open my drawer and grab a high necked t-shirt and sweats, and rush to the bathroom to slip them on. He can be so gentle at times. I've heard the saying "kill you with kindness". That's Danny. He hides his evil in kindness.

"Here, get in bed and try to sleep, beautiful."

He hands me a hot water bottle as I leave the bathroom.

I smile. "Thanks."

I crawl into the bed, the chilled sheets making me shiver.

"Cold? Let me warm you up."

He pulls me against his chest, holding me tight to his body and all I can think about is tomorrow. I'll be free of him. Sammy's going to have a plan.

Blaydon's horrified bellow wakes me from slumber. I struggle with the covers as I scramble to get to him; Danny is already opening the bedroom door to exit when I detangle myself. My stomach drops when I make it to the hallway and find Blaydon pointing to his room, shaking his head. "She's fucking dead!"

I take a deep breath and follow Danny into Blaydon's room. There, lying naked in Blay's bed, is Maria. She's a funny colour, unnatural. Danny checks her pulse and curses.

I turn to Blay meeting him on the floor "Must be an overdose," I mutter, though it sounds more like a question then a statement.

"She wasn't on anything, just booze, River! Oh my God, did I do this?"

I shake my head and grasp his cheeks in a firm hold, making him look at me. His glassy eyes break my heart. I'm vibrating with adrenaline. "No way, Blaydon. You would never hurt anyone."

He looks at me the pain his feeling seeps into me from his watery gaze. "I would, I did!"

"That was different, Blay. You didn't do this."

He didn't do this, he couldn't, and I refuse to believe anything else. I need to help him. Save him, protect him.

He shudders and a tear escapes his eye.

"What the fuck do we do?" Danny asks.

I stand up. "You need to help him, Danny. Get rid of her." Blaydon gasps and I add, "I can't lose him over her overdosing, Danny!"

Danny watches me intently.

"She didn't overdose," Blay whispers. "She didn't take anything."

I scan Danny's face and give him a gentle nod.

"It was an overdose, Blaydon," Danny says. "Some of my stash is missing. She probably crept out while we were sleeping."

I thank him with my eyes. Blaydon exhales a ragged breath.

"I'm doing this for you, River. Tell me you love me."

I swallow my hate; I swallow my love for Sammy, and I swallow my freedom.

"I love you. Please, Danny, help him."

He drops a chaste kiss to my lips. "Take Blaydon to our room and stay there until I come for you."

I turn, dragging Blaydon to his feet and down the hall to my room. I guide him to the bed and climb in behind him, holding him while he cries.

CHAPTER TWENTY-THREE
Sammy

I plan to go to my dad's, to get him to sign all the money from my gran over to me so I can get everything in motion. Today, I'll sit down and tell River that she's moving in with me and leaving Danny. I'll tell him myself since I know he has a temper. I'll come to blows with him, but she's more than worth it. My phone pings with a text alert from Derek, telling me he can meet me later. I reply, letting him know it's no longer necessary. I text River, asking her to come over when she wakes up.

I can't come over, Sammy. This isn't what I want anymore. I'm sorry.

I read and then re-read about twenty times, my brain not accepting the words.

What? What's happened between now and last night?

I can't talk now.

She can't talk now? What the fuck? My heart is beating at a rapid rate. This can't be happening, she loves me. I felt it in her touch, I saw it in her eyes, and she fucking told me with her own lips. I throw my phone and it lands on the sofa. I see Danny out the corner of my eye, walking from his car. He has a big smile on his face that I want to punch off. I open the front door and drop down the front steps. "Why are you so happy?" I ask.

He grins, looking up at River's house before hushing me back towards mine. He pulls a black box from his pocket and cracks the lid. I feel the colour drain from my face.

"You sure she'll say yes?"

He snaps the box shut and pushes my shoulder. "Gee thanks, man. She's already said yes, I just went to get the ring from the jeweller."

I'm having motherfucking heart failure at twenty-two. I'm standing here dying, my heart squeezing the life from me.

"Sammy, you look like you're going to pass out. It's me getting hitched, not you!"

God, she said she was broken, but so am I and she just gave Danny the power to wield the hammer that shattered me into a million pieces.

"Congrats, man." I turn and rush up the stairs, go straight into the study and crack open a bottle of Jack, and chug it back.

"Sam, what the fuck, man?"

I crack my eyelids and wince from the light. "Go away," I croak.

"I've been looking for you all day. I thought you went out. It's six o'clock!"

I must have passed out after finishing the bottle. I've been in here eight hours. The room spins as I sit up.

"I need you to drive me to my dad's."

Jasper eyes focus on me, questions creasing his brow "What's going on, Sam?"

I shake my head and instantly regret it when my skull begins a dull thud. I shuffle past Jasper to the kitchen, blast the cold tap, and wrap my lips around it, swallowing the water down my parched throat. That's when I see her, like an angel, spinning her body around on her deck. It's raining heavily but she doesn't seem to even notice as it beats against her body. I wrench the back door open and shout over the fence, "Twink, get out here, now!"

I walk to the front yard and wait for her to come through the gate, the rain soaking through my clothes in seconds.

CHAPTER TWENTY-FOUR
River

The rain is pouring down, drumming against the ground, causing Sammy to shout to enable me to hear him. He looks beautiful but broken, just like me. He's hurting, and I hate that it's me who made him hurt.

"I know you're scared, Twink, but I love you and I know you love me, too. We didn't fuck last night, we made love."

My soaked summer dress clings to my body, my weathered hair sticks to my cheeks, my salty tears mixing with the rain that's battering against me.

"Just breathe, Twink, and let me love you. Step into the future with me, and leave everything else in your past. Come to me, baby."

He's holding his hand out to me across the small edge of the grass separating our houses.

"It's not that simple, Sammy." The words come out choked and his eyes plead with me.

"We were meant to be together. You know it, Twink. I don't know what happened with Danny all those years ago, but I know I shouldn't have just walked away. I should have come to you. I didn't then and it killed me for four fucking years. I won't do it again. I belong to you. You own me River, and I feel it when we're together. I own you, too."

My heart is breaking because he's right. He owns my heart, my soul. But Danny owns my conscience. He keeps me prisoner with the knowledge he has on Blaydon, and he'll use it against me if I leave him.

"I'll tell Danny," Sammy says. "You don't have to face this on your own."

Panic sears through me. "No! No, don't say anything to Danny. I will."

His body relaxes, his shoulders dropping as he nods his head. "You're going to tell him and be with me?"

I don't answer. He waltzes towards me, cupping my cheeks and crushing his lips fiercely to mine. "You're going to be with me, River. Every day I'm going to show you how much I love you. Say yes, baby. Say yes."

I want to drown in him, let the rain wash away those four years we missed out on and drown us in each other, but Danny holds so much more power now. He used Maria's death to bribe me to marry him, to be trapped forever. God, the emptiness is creeping its way back in, stripping me of the fragments Sammy had put back together. Blaydon wouldn't survive in prison and I couldn't live knowing he was there. This is such a mess.

Sammy's hands grip mine, then he looks down and steps back.

"You really did say yes to him."

I look down to the diamond Danny put on my finger.

"Something bad happened, Sammy."

The rain washes down our faces, dripping into my mouth as I speak. Sammy's body is shaking, steam billowing from his heated skin from the cold contrast of the rain.

"You're right. Something bad *did* happen. I let you back into my fucking heart, River. I let myself love you. I'm so done. I can't be here watching you marry him."

He turns to leave and I feel my head spin. "Sammy! Please, you don't understand!"

He stops but doesn't turn around. "I've never understood, River!" he roars, leaving me on my own to my fate. The fate Danny claimed those four years ago. I drop to my knees and let the rain drown me in my misery.

Four painful weeks have passed. I can't eat without getting sick, I can't breathe without my heart constricting, bleeding for my lost love. I haven't seen or heard from Sammy. Blaydon is falling deeper into depression. He's hardly left his room, and he isn't showing up for work. Danny is on top of the world, though. He keeps trying to talk to me about setting a wedding date, but I can't even fake smiles for him anymore. I lost everything I was; my soul left with Sammy. Jasper came home a few days ago. He told me Sammy's staying with his dad, but he's coming home soon for business. I don't know what I'll say to him when he comes back, nothing has changed. I'm still trapped by the knowledge Danny has. I'm fading into nothing. Soon I'll just be mist, an apparition of the girl who once lived here inside me. I haven't even been dancing. Bella sold Bella's, and closed its doors, its future uncertain. I can't even face dancing out the back because it reminds me of Sammy taking me on the platform.

"Hey."

I look up from the desk. I've been at work for three hours, and still not done anything. My eyes collide with Derek's. He's in a fitted suit, his badge sitting on his left hip, a gun on his right.

"Hey," I say.

"You okay? You look tired."

"I'm fine. What are you doing here?"

He looks around then brings his eyes back to mine. "I'm actually here to ask you a few questions."

I sit up straighter in my seat, nerves beginning to eat away at my insides. "What about?"

He pulls a picture from his back pocket and hands it to me. "Do you recognise her?"

God, I'm looking at a picture of Maria.

"Yeah, I saw her at a party a few weeks ago."

He raises a brow. "And what about with Danny or Blaydon?"

I swallow, even though my mouth is bone dry. "What's this about?"

He slips the photo back in his pocket. "She was found dead at a crack house down town a few weeks ago."

I try to look shocked, but I can tell I'm not fooling him. "Well, that's a shame. A lot of people turn to drugs to cope these days."

He nods. "Yeah, but she was clean. She died from suffocation."

A cold dread creeps up my spine. Blay would never do that, it must have been an accident.

"River, are you okay?"

Oh my God, how long have I been sitting, frozen? Derek is kneeling at my feet, holding my hands.

"I'm sorry, it's just weird after seeing her, and now she's dead."

He strokes my hand. "River, I need to ask you something else."

I feel the fear like it's a living entity, consuming me. "What?"

"Do you know anything about the disappearance of Mr Knight?"

I blink a few times, confused. "Danny?"

"Danny's father. Mrs Knight said he left the house last month and never came back. Now, this does happen as you're well aware. People leave without a word, start fresh somewhere else, but I need to investigate all reports."

He went on business with Danny. I don't understand, Danny hasn't mentioned anything.

"Have you spoken to Danny?" I ask.

He stands, towering over me. "That's my next stop. Listen, River, I just want you to know that if you do know anything about anything, and you're scared, I will protect you. I'll do everything I can for you."

Tears brim my lashes without permission as I look up at Derek. Can he help me? Would he help Blaydon? My mouth opens to speak when Stevie interrupts, saving me from making a mistake.

"River, sweetheart, you need to order these parts." He hands me a list. "Oh, hey," he adds, noticing Derek.

"Hey. River, take my card. I've written my personal number on the back. Call me anytime, I'll be in touch."

I watch as he walks across the forecourt to his car.

"Everything okay, sweetheart?" Stevie asks.

I give him a smile. "Yeah, fine."

I stare at Derek's card until the numbers blur together.

"Hi." My eyes shoot up to find the smiling face of Jasper.

"Hi back."

He points to my bag. "Grab your purse, we're going to lunch."

We sit in the same diner he, Sammy and I came to the first time they showed up to take me to lunch.

"He's a mess."

I peel my eyes from the menu I'm pretending to scan and look up to Jasper's serious gaze. I've never seen this side of him.

"I really like you. I can see why he loves you, but you're killing him, River. He was a mess when I met him and it took a lot to pull him back, but this time it's so much worse. He's heartbroken."

Tears pour freely from my eyes, the burn a welcome pain. "I love him so much, Jasper, but it's so complicated. There's a reason I'm still with Danny, and it's not because I chose him over Sammy."

He reaches across the table to grasp my closed fist. "Help me understand because you're not making sense. Are you afraid of Danny? Because me and Sammy will keep you safe."

A sob breaks free and I know people are staring at us. "Can you drop me somewhere? I don't trust myself driving in this state."

He squeezes my hand. "Of course. Let's get some food in you first, though. You look slimmer. Are you eating?"

I shake my head.

I make Jasper drop me at Derek's after he fed me. I send a text to Derek, letting him know I'm at his house, and he messages me back, telling me to go in and make myself at home. He'll be at least an hour.

His place is warm and inviting, despite the size. The dark wooden floors throughout, and warm rich colours remind me of a posh library. I sit down on his oversized leather couch and wait.

The scent of coffee invades my nose. My eyes blink open to see Derek standing there, holding a mug.

"Hey." I rub my eyes and sit up. There's a heavy blanket laid over me. "I'm sorry, I must have drifted off. I've been tired lately."

He smiles warmly. "It's not a problem. I put the blanket on you and left you for a few hours."

My mouth drops open. "A few hours?" He hands me the steaming mug and I inhale the scent. "Thank you."

He walks to the chair opposite and sits. "I'm glad you came here, but I didn't expect to see you this soon."

I remove the blanket from my legs as I scoot forward on the seat, holding up the mug so I don't spill hot coffee on my lap.

"Can I trust you Derek?" I ask, in a soft whisper.

He mirrors my pose and drops his head to look into my eyes. "Yes, River. I swear I'll protect you."

I swallow. "Why?"

He asked me out for dinner so he must find me attractive, but he doesn't really know me, so I have to know why he would help me.

He sits back. "Why what?"

"Why would you help me?"

His eyes scan my body, making me squirm. "I was drawn to you when I first saw you. You're a beautiful girl. I won't lie and say I don't hope you will consider losing the overbearing ass, and let me treat you how you should be treated, but I know I wouldn't be the one you turn to if you did leave him."

I sip my coffee and soak in this information.

"You remind me of someone I lost a long time ago. I couldn't help her, but I can help you if you'll let me."

I scan his face but only see truth in his eyes. "Why couldn't you help her?"

"I didn't see how far gone she was."

He exhales and looks down at his hands. "My little sister, she was eighteen, and head over heels for this older, abusive man. He used her and smacked her around. When I saw the bruises, I confronted him. As punishment for her telling me, he fucked her best friend, filmed it, and sent it to her." His voice wavers. "She killed herself that night." He rubs his hands through his hair. "I've never told anyone that. I felt responsible for her as her big brother to protect her. My mom blamed me for confronting the boyfriend. She hasn't spoken to me since the day of her funeral. I know you have no one. I see the grief and loneliness in your eyes."

I reach for his hand. "I have Blay. He means everything to me." I take a deep breath. "If someone committed a crime, and someone else helped them cover it, would they both be in trouble?"

He studies my face before he speaks. "It depends what role they played in the cover up. Knowing of a crime and being too scared to tell anyone is not a crime."

"What if someone helped get rid of the evidence of the crime?"

"Yes, that is a crime, River."

"What if the crime was an accident, or self-defence?"

He reaches up and tucks a lock of my hair behind my ear. "Then that changes things."

I squeeze his hand and hold onto him for hope. "If I asked you to help someone for me, would you?"

He looks down at my hand holding his. "River, you're not making much sense, but of course. If you tell me whatever happened was self-defence or an accident I'll help, but you need to start talking because you've not actually told me anything."

I release his hand. "I know and I'm sorry. I just need to speak to my brother first. Can I come back tomorrow and maybe bring him with me?"

He stands and embraces me. "That's fine, River."

"Thank you, Derek."

He squeezes me, then releases me and I begin to fidget.

"Would you be able to take me back to the garage? I left my car there. I got a ride here."

He grins. "That's fine. Can I entice you to eat with me first?"

I bite down on my lip. "I really need to get back. I'm sorry, another time, though."

"It's fine, River. Come, let me drive you to your car."

He opens the door for me when we reach his car. I slide into the passenger seat and jump when he leans over me with the seat belt. I grab it from his hand. "I can do it."

He looks amused and holds up his hands. "It's just that seat belt is-" Before he can finish I try to click the belt in place but it springs free and pulls back at a rapid rate, burning along my neck. "Broken. Shit, are you okay?" He pulls the collar of my shirt down slightly and winces. "That's going to bruise."

I lean forward and flip the mirror to look at the deep red mark on my neck and shoulder.

"Don't worry, I'll put some cream on it when I get home."

Derek reaches for the belt and pulls it over me, clicking it in place with a hard tug.

"Thank you."

The drive to the lot is a quiet one and I'm grateful he doesn't ask me more questions. Everyone has left when we pull up; I missed most of the afternoon. I thank Derek and promise to stop by tomorrow. I head to my car and close my eyes. I need to speak to Blaydon to see if he'll tell Derek everything, to see what our options are. The ride home is a fuzzy memory as I sit outside our house, not remembering driving here. I grab my purse and make my way indoors.

"Blay, you home?" I call out, throwing my purse down on the couch. I walk to his room, but I'm pulled backwards by my ponytail. My hands fly up to grip the hand that has me in a vice-like grip. Danny's cold, deadly voice pierces my ear. "Did you fuck him?"

He drags me down the hall to our room and shoves me forward. I turn to face him, but I wish I hadn't because what I see terrifies me. His face is contorted in anger.

"I went to pick you up at lunch, but guess what Stevie happily informed me? That pretty boy took you to lunch! I waited all fucking day for you, but you never came back so I drove home. Blaydon said you hadn't been here, so where were you?" he screams in my face, his hands gripping my throat, pinning me against the wall.

They say you have a limit, that when you reach it you just can't take anymore. I thought mine disintegrated, washed away years ago in the tide of disappointment and misery abandoning me to keep on suffering for eternity. But this was it. I just felt myself snap, I couldn't bare this lie one more second.

"I hate you," I breathe.

He flinches and steps back. "What?"

I can't take it anymore. I can't take living this lie, feeling this empty. "I hate you!" I scream. "If it wasn't for Blaydon I wouldn't be with you! He is the only reason I let myself live in this misery!"

"You love me!"

"No, I don't!"

"River, are you okay?" I hear Blaydon through the door and I cover my mouth with a shaky hand. Did he hear all of that? Oh, God, I don't want him to know I'm only with Danny to protect him. He would rather hand himself in than let me be unhappy.

"I'm fine, Blay," I manage to call out in a calm voice.

"You sure?"

"She said she's fine, Blay! Go pop some pills or something!"

I slap Danny hard across the face. The red hand print on his cheek sends terror into my veins. Oh, God, he will kill me.

His hand shoots out and grips my throat again. I hear Blay's boots carry down the hall. I close my eyes and wait for the darkness, but it doesn't come. I open my eyes and see Danny staring at my neck. He rips the collar of my top from my neck and shoulder.

"What the fuck?" He grabs me, yanking me forward. "You fucking cunt!"

I gasp. Danny has never spoken to me with such animosity before.

"Like it rough, River? Is that it? Have I been doing it wrong all these years?" He throws me down hard, my head colliding with the dresser. A painful burn explodes in my head and I feel the warm trickle of blood. Danny's frame comes over mine, immobilizing me, his hand covering my mouth and nose.

"I can do rough, River."

He tears at my clothes and I sob behind his hand, struggling for breath. My stomach protests and I start retching. He removes his hand and his weight from my body. I turn my head and expel the contents of my stomach onto the carpet.

Danny grabs me under the arm and lifts me into our en-suite where I vomit over the toilet. "It's from a seat belt."

"What?"

I point to the mark on my neck, feeling dizzy from the cut on my head. "The mark is from a seat belt burn."

He paces the bathroom. "I will kill him, River. I will end any fucking man you even think about, do you understand me? I will kill him!"

I sob as the images of Sammy dead at Danny's hand assault

my mind. I need to end this. I try to stand, but black out instead.

"River, you scared the shit out of me!"

I lift my heavy head. I'm in the car with Danny. "Where are we going?"

He looks at me then back to the road. "Hospital. You need stiches. You fainted and banged the back of your head in the fall."

I don't know who he's trying to convince, me or him. *Yeah, that's what happened, asshole.* He must have sensed my thoughts.

"That's what happened. Don't fuck with me, River. I have no problem telling the cops what happened to Maria and your father."

I turn and narrow my eyes. "You helped him. If he goes down, so do you."

He shrugs. "So?"

I deflate. He doesn't care about facing prison because he's evil enough to survive it. Blaydon's not. He wouldn't cope in prison.

We pull up at the hospital and Danny helps me out of the car. He stays by my side constantly. The nurse station is a flurry of activity; patients and doctors coming and going. I'm handed a form to fill in, and told to take a seat. Danny is seething mad that they're not seeing to me above everyone else. After a gruelling wait, a nurse calls my name and guides me to a gurney with a curtain around it. A doctor, a tall man with dark skin and warm brown eyes, slips through the curtain.

"Hello, I'm Doctor King. Can you tell me why you're here?"

"She fainted and banged her head in the fall," Danny informs him. "I wrote it on the form you make injured patients fill out, even with a head injury."

The doctor doesn't seem fazed by Danny's hostility. "Were you with her at the time, sir?"

Danny glares at him. "I found her."

"Do you know how long you were unconscious?"

I fidget on the bed. "An hour," I murmur.

He looks down at his chart before dropping it on the foot of the bed. He snaps some gloves on and shines a light in my eyes. He holds up a finger and makes me follow it with my eyes, then smiles and brushes the hair away from the gash on my head. "Okay, you need some stiches, and we want to take a urine sample and a blood sample to see what made you faint in the first place. Is there a possibility you could be pregnant?"

I pale, a sick stirring rolling my stomach, the risk of pregnancy had never been an issue. Danny answers for me. "She can't be. I can't have children. I contracted measles when I was young and it left me infertile."

The doctor looks to me. "Okay, well we will test anyway. It's just routine. I'll send the nurse in to collect a sample and to deal with the stitches."

I nod, take the small pot from his hand and go into the bathroom. I deposit the required sample. The nurse is waiting for me when I come out.

"This one doesn't take long, but the blood samples will be a few days."

She takes my sample and leaves. A different nurse comes in, pulling a trolley with medical equipment on it.

"I'll be outside while you do that," Danny says when he sees her pick up a needle.

She laughs. "Is he queasy?"

I tell her yes, even though he isn't. I have no idea why he suddenly left me alone. The nurse holds my arm out and taps at the crease in the middle of my arm. "You'll feel a pinch."

She inserts the needle and my blood fills the vial attached to it. Once she's done, she labels the vial then picks up a sterile wipe to wipe down the wound on my head before injecting some liquid to numb the area. She doesn't take long to stitch up the gash.

"I'll just get this cleared and see if the urine sample showed up anything."

I raise an eyebrow. "That quick?"

She laughs. "We have a stick for lots of different things. We just dip them in for a minute and get answers."

I nod my head and smile as she leaves.

Danny flies into the room. "Get up we're leaving."

I stand from the bed. "What? Why?"

He grabs my forearm. "Because I fucking said so, River. We've been here for hours waiting. You're stitched up, they can phone the results from the tests."

Danny's scary when he's on edge so I let him drag me out of the hospital.

We pull up to our house but he doesn't turn the ignition off. "Go inside and pack a bag."

My stomach plummets. "Why?"

He doesn't answer, he just growls at me so I leap from the car and run up the path to our house. I fumble for the door, turning to watch completely baffled as to why Danny drives away. I close the door, resting my head on the frame.

"Blay, we need to talk!" I call out, feeling de ja vu from earlier. I check behind me out of instinct but no one's there.

"Blay?" I push his door open.

I must have died. I'm the living dead. My body is breathing but I'm no longer alive.

Blay is pale as a ghost, his head tipped back onto his mattress, his lifeless body propped up against the bed on the floor, both wrists sliced open. Pools of blood stain the carpet. I run to him, but I know it's too late. No one can bleed that much and still be alive. I lift my shaking fingers to his neck. No pulse.

"Oh, God, no," I sob. "Why did you leave me, Blaydon?"

I scream, pain like a million shards of glass cutting into my heart tears through me. My life is bleeding out in my tears, my reason for living, the reason I condemned myself to Danny's torture is gone, and he left me just like everyone else. Anger consumes me manifesting itself with in me. Why did he do this? How could he leave me just like she did? My father's voice echoes in my memory:

"Your mother hated her fuck up of a son, so she sliced and diced herself until there was no blood left inside her. It's just us now."

I was twelve years old, and that's how he told me my mother was gone. Sammy was my lifeline back then, but he's left me again. I have no one and Danny would kill Sammy if he knew I loved him. My whole life is one disaster after another, I just want out. I look up at the grey face of my once loving brother and notice a note next to his head with my name on it. I reach for it with shaky hands.

River,

I'm so sorry. I know you would never want this for me, and how much pain me following Mum will cause you but I'm doing it for the opposite reasons. I'm doing this to protect you, to give you freedom. I heard you and Danny arguing. I know you're only with him to protect me. I can't tell you how much I wish you had a better childhood. It was dark and painful and it lives inside me, Riv. I can't find any peace, it follows me everywhere. I can't suppress it; it chokes me, even in my dreams. Sometimes I feel him hitting me. I see him in the shadows, taunting me. I dream he crawls inside me, poisoning my blood. I know I'm fucked up, Riv. I know it's all in my mind, and I try to cut him out, I try to block him out but he lives in me. I'm bound by his torture, by our past, by the deaths, the ghosts all around us. I just want to find quiet. I'm tired of being here. I'm tired of breathing but not living. These wounds will never heal, no amount of time can erase the memories I live every day. Please leave Danny and be with Sammy. He loves you, Riv, he has always loved you and you deserve to be loved, to feel and give love. You were the only person who loved me and I want to thank you for that. Thank you for loving me and giving me something to love, because I have someone to watch over now, and I will I'll watch over you, Riv, always. I love you sister of mine,

Love Blay

The agony inside me is unbearable. I couldn't save him, just like, deep down, he never really saved me. I went from a victim of one predator to the victim of another. Danny stole my innocence. He stole what could have been with Sammy. I won't let him take anything else. He does love me in his sick, fucked up way, and if I died it would hurt him. It would end this.

I stand and go to the boot of my car. I pull the gas can with extra gas in case of emergencies and carry it through the back yard. I pour it in a circle around the wooden platform, then throw the empty can down and go back inside. I pocket Blay's lighter and bend down next to him. I drag him from his bedroom, falling on my ass a couple of times in the process. He weighs a ton and his blood is leaving a trail, making me heave and sob as I drag him through the kitchen into the back yard. I place him in the centre of the circle and pause to catch my breath. Dusk has cast a dark shadow over everything, the sun offering its last soft orange glow in the horizon. I take my phone from my pocket to ring Sammy's cell, and I'm relieved when his answer phone kicks in:

"It's Sammy, you know what to do!"

"Hey Sammy, it's me, River. I know you're hurting right now

and I'm so sorry for that. I want you to know I love you. I've always loved you, ever since I watched you break down through the hole in the fence on the first day you moved here. You fit in, Sammy. You matched me. I was broken, too. I watched my dad beat my brother while my mom did nothing to protect him. Blay was my hero. He saved me so many times from the hands of our dad. On my sixteenth birthday, Blay killed him to protect me. Our dad had become more touchy-feely the older I got. He was a sick man, Sammy. He was obsessed with me. My mom saw it and killed herself instead of taking me and Blaydon away from him. Danny walked in on us the night of my sixteenth and helped Blaydon bury him in the garden." A small laugh rips from my chest. "Blaydon built me the platform so I could dance on his grave. The thing is, Blay did stop our dad from coming to my room that night but he didn't know how to stop Danny coming in his place. He stole my innocence that night while I cried and thought of you. He told me I belonged to him. I would have done anything to protect Blaydon. I wish someone had saved us both. I wished you would come for me but you left, and I died inside. You own my soul, Sammy, but Danny will never let me breathe so I'm following my brother to find peace. Peace we couldn't find here in the darkness of our past. I love you always."

I end the call and tap out a message to Derek.

Our father's in a grave in my back yard. Maria was an accident. Danny dumped her body. Arrest him and make him pay. For what you find here, I'm sorry, Derek.

My phone begins to chirp but I ignore it. I cradle my brother and slip the lighter from my pocket.

"What are you doing?"

My breath stutters. I didn't see Jasper approach.

"Oh my God. River, is he dead?"

I hold up my hand. "Stay back, Jasper."

That's when I see Danny come through the back door. He fists his hand and ploughs it straight into Jasper's face, knocking him to the ground.

"Jasper!"

"That stupid fuck. I can't believe he killed himself." Danny laughs with malice, looking at Blaydon. "Drop him and come here, River. Now."

I shake my head. "He couldn't live with what he did!"

Danny laughs again. "He was a stupid fuck. He didn't even kill anybody."

What is he talking about? He killed our father. My mind battles; memories from that night engulf me.

I hear muffled moans and a low thump, thump, thump. My heart rate spikes and my eyes fly open. I pull back the covers and tiptoe to my bedroom door. I push the side of my face flat against the cold wood, straining to hear. THUMP! My door rattles, vibrating against my head, pushing me back.

"No, no, please don't!" I hear Blay cry. The door handle pushes down. The shadow of my father creeps across my bedroom carpet with the light from the hall way, highlighting him like the boogie man in nightmares. I step back, shaking; my eyes find a broken and battered Blaydon lying on the floor, and a small sob cracks from my chest.

"Blay."

My dad's angry gaze turns to him so quickly he almost seems inhuman. "You fucking stay out there!" he warns, and my eyes go wide as he steps into my room and closes the door. He walks towards me. "Come lay down with Daddy, my beautiful girl."

He lifts an empty bottle of whiskey to his lips and shakes it. "Huh," he huffs. "Go get Daddy another bottle, beautiful. Then I want to hold you for a while, and show you how much Daddy loves you." He walks closer and strokes a hand down my face. "You look like your Mama when I first met her. So beautiful.”

I reach for the empty bottle and slowly walk from the room, shaking with every step. I walk down the hall into the kitchen.

“Blay,” I say to his back. He’s standing, frozen. I step around him and gasp at the carving knife he’s holding. I put the empty bottle down on the table and slip my hand into his, taking the knife from him.

“I won’t let him do it, River. I’ve kept him from your room all these years. I won’t let him I won’t let him, I won’t let him.”

I reach to cup his face. “I know, Blay. Thank you,” I whisper, bringing his head down to cradle him.

“You little cunt! Go to your room!” our father shouts, grabbing the back of Blaydon’s shirt and yanking him from me. He kicks him down the hall then turns back to me, closing the distance in a few short strides. His hand comes crashing down across my face, my head whips to the side from the impact and I stumble a few paces.

“He’s the reason your mama killed herself and yet you still give him all your affection.”

He reaches for me and crushes me to him, his grip tight.

A loud crack rings out into the quiet of the night, and Dad’s grip loosens. He falls to the floor. Dark liquid oozes from underneath his head, forming a puddle, his sin-filled blood leaking in a red river of Karma. I tear my eyes from the still form of our father to see Blay standing there, holding the empty whisky bottle. “Oh my God. I killed him.”

The knuckle rap on the back door makes us both jump.

“I called Danny earlier,” Blay whispers, his eyes widening as the door handle dips and Danny steps into the kitchen.

“Hey, you ready?” he spoke casually, then his eyes take in the scene in front of him and he runs a hand through his hair. “Oh shit. What the fuck happened?”

Blay begins to cough, wincing, and red fluid spatters from his mouth onto his hand.

“Blay, shit, man,” Danny says, going to him.

"My ribs again. Fuck, I killed him Dan."

Danny looks to the still form on the floor, a sneer turning his handsome face into a scary grimace.

"He was protecting me," I mutter. Danny strides to me and tips my face to the side; my cheek is on fire from where my dad had hit me.

"He fucking hit you." His tone is deadly.

"Yeah," I whisper, a small sob escaping my parted lips.

"Take your brother to the bathroom, wrap his ribs. I'll figure out what to do, come up with a story."

"Is he dead?" Blay's panicking biting his nails and shaking his head.

"Take your brother, River."

I rush to Blaydon and force him down the hall into the bathroom. In his room I lift his shirt and flinch. His stomach is black and blue with bruises. I run my hands over old scars. "I'm so sorry, Blaydon." Tears fall from my eyes.

"Hey, don't, Riv."

I shake my head. "No, Blay! Half of these scars and bruises are from you protecting me."

He lowers his head to look into my eyes. "River you're my baby sister. You're the only person who has ever loved me, and I'll always protect you. I love you sister of mine."

I grab the bandages from the drawer and wrap his ribs in silence.

"Why are you holding shovels?" My voice breaks because I know the answer.

"He's dead, so we bury him or Blay goes to prison for life." Danny places the shovels on the kitchen table and comes over to me, cupping my face. "Do you want that?"

I shake my head, furiously. "No! No, I can't lose him no, no, no!"

Danny pulls me against his chest. "Shh, it's okay, Riv. I'll help him for you." He pulls back and stares into my eyes. "For you, okay?"

A sob breaks free. "Thank you, Danny," I whisper.

"Go to your room, River. I'll take care of this."

I step around Blaydon and run to my room, closing the door and collapsing into my bed.

"He was bleeding. There was so much blood," I murmur.

Danny scoffs. "Head injuries bleed a lot, he had a strong pulse."

I cradle Blay's limp, cold body into my chest. "Did you bury him alive?"

He rolls his eyes. "No, when you went to wrap Blay's ribs, I smothered him. Thing with intoxication, Riv, it can leave you defenceless, ask Maria. Oh wait, you can't."

My breath hitches. "Did you kill her too, Danny?"

"She wasn't worth the fucking air she was breathing. Do you know she dropped her panties to try and get me to fuck her?" He sneers. "She was a disgusting whore who spoke trash about you, and she used your brother and tried to fuck your man."

A tear escapes to my cheek. "You're not my man, Danny. You're a murderer."

"Tsk tsk, tsk. Be careful, River. I heard you with Blaydon, talking about me not being able to hold your father's death over you, so I decided to give you another incentive. Playing Blay was easy. He was always so out of his face on sleeping pills, he didn't even feel me smother his girlfriend while she thrashed next to him." He raises his leg and swings it forward into Jasper's stomach. "I'll always be your man. You think I'll ever let you go, or let some pretty boy take you from me? I'll fucking kill him. I'll kill him, River! You belong to me!" He bellows, and I vibrate with fear.

"I have nothing now, Danny. Blaydon was the only reason I was with you and he's gone."

He paces, pulling tufts of his hair he reaches into the back of his jeans pulling a gun and tapping the end of a gun to his head. Oh God, he has a gun. "What about him? I'll let him go if you come with me." He points the gun at Jasper.

I shake my head. "I don't care about him, Danny," I bluff, hoping I sound confident.

He grins and points the gun at Jasper. "You sure about that?"

I flip the lighter open. I raise it up and a gunshot rings out; a high pitched noise pierces my ears. It's my scream.

"It's a stomach wound, you have time to get him help, River."

I flip the lighter down and the flame sparks. I throw the lighter, engulfing a circle of flames around me and Blaydon on the raised platform.

"River! River!"

I hear Sammy's voice bleed through my sobs. I watch in horror as he rushes through the gate, and runs up the steps. He stills as Danny points the gun at his face.

"Sorry you had to see this, bro," Danny tells him. Sammy's eyes fall to Jasper, he blanches then turns to me, and then Blaydon.

"River," his voice is small and choked with agony.

"Sammy, you weren't meant to be back until tomorrow!"

I can't compose myself. My heart and head are broken. Blaydon lays dead in my arms, Jasper beaten and shot, and Danny holds a gun at the only man I've ever loved.

"Danny, don't hurt her. Please let me get to her."

My heart sinks further at Sammy's words. I know Danny won't take that well and the cracking sound that follows proves me right. Sammy's grunting, and then his knees hit the floor, making me panic.

"No, Danny! Please! I'll go with you."

His face contorts into pure hatred, and he hits himself in the head with the handle of the gun. "It's fucking Sammy, isn't it? I should have known you always had a thing for him, but I thought this pretty boy turned your head!"

"Danny, no! No, please I'll be with you. I love you!"

He looks at me through the growing flames. "Move away from the fire, River, or you'll kill more than just yourself."

I look at Sammy. "Promise me you won't hurt them anymore," I beg.

He sneers. "Fine, if you won't come to me." He raises the gun and shoots Sammy.

"No!" I drop Blaydon; the fire is becoming too intense. I feel the heat all over my body; it's a hot, deadly wall keeping me from getting to Sammy. I feel like I moved outside my own life, I'm a spectator on the side lines watching in. my mind trying to refuses any more trauma. If someone could die from heartache the bullet fired at Sammy would have made me ash floating away on the wind. Danny disappears, and then reappears with Blaydon's mattress. He throws it down in front of me, quashing the flames. He grabs me and drags me away from the fire and through the house.

"Did you pack a bag?"

"No!" I shriek, trying to get free from his hold. He raises the gun, bringing it down heavily against my head, submerging me in darkness.

CHAPTER TWENTY-FIVE
Sammy

I haven't seen her for four long, painful weeks. How am I going to move on, knowing she's marrying him? Knowing she chose him again. God, this bottle was full an hour ago, now it's empty and I can still feel. Why am not I numb yet? Jasper called to say he picked up the keys for Bella's; I bought it for her. I was hoping to talk Blaydon into letting me help run the garage so River could have her own studio, but then she let Danny put a ring on her finger. How could she let me touch her, kiss her soft skin, stroke her body and be inside her if she didn't want to be with me? God, now all I can think about is being inside her tight, warm body; she's ruined me for anyone else. I've been with some dirty chicks, chicks down for anything, and some good girls that just wanted to let loose for a night, but I've never experienced a girl like River. She was raw, real, beautiful and passionate. God, I still have the marks on my back. They're faint scars, but they're still there and they always will be. Our passion embedded in my skin forever. Fuck, I can still smell her sweet scent if I close my eyes and picture her. I fucking miss her. I need another bottle.

"Sammy, someone's on the phone for you. He says it's important."

I scrub my hands down my face and roll onto my back, the effects from drinking the night before pumps into my brain. I stand up with a grumble about being woken up early when I notice the time. Six p.m. I've slept eighteen hours.

I snatch the phone from my dad. "Hello." I sound groggy as fuck.

"Sammy, its Blay." I reach for the glass from my dad's hand and give him a head tilt as thanks. "What's up, Blay?"

"It's River."

I sigh. "Listen, Blay. I can't talk to you about her, man."

I hear his heavy breathing down the line. "She loves you, Sammy, and she needs you. She's really going to need you. Don't let her stay with him. She loves you, Sammy. Look after her for me."

The dial tone buzzes down the line

"Blay? Blay!"

I dial River's mobile but get no answer. I try Blaydon's and Danny's. Nothing. Panic, that's what I'm feeling right now. Blay sounded weird. What the fuck is going on? I rush out of the room and through the house.

"Dad, I need to go. I'll call."

I jump in my car, start her up and hit the road. I keep trying everyone's phone and eventually get Jasper.

"Dude, I'm fucking busy. Fucking being the operative word." He chuckles.

"I need you to do me a favour."

I hear a giggle in the background. "Yeah, I'm a little busy, man."

"A lot busy," some chick croons down the phone.

"Fucking hell, Jasper! Listen, I need you to go over to River's and check shit out."

I hear a shuffling of movement.

"Why, is she okay?"

"I don't know. Blaydon phoned me being really weird over two hours ago. I need you to check on River. I'm on my way home."

"I'm getting dressed now, man, but I'm over an hour away. I'm with some chick I met."

"I'm about the same distance. Just meet me there, Jasp. I'm freaking out."

I hear a door close.

"I'm leaving now."

I end the call and break a few speed laws. I pick my phone up again to call River, but it's dead and I've left my charger at my dad's.

When I pull up, I see everyone's cars here, including Jasper's. I smell smoke and hear muffled voices coming from the back of River's house. I follow the smoke to River's back yard, and stop short.

Flames surround her, and she's kneeling, holding Blaydon. He's a vile, grey colour. I rush up the steps and come nose to nose with a muzzle of a gun. I let my eyes travel the length, seeing Danny is the one holding it. That's when I notice Jasper lying, bleeding. There's so much blood staining his shirt. My mind is struggling to cope. What's happening? Everything is happening so fast. Words are spoken, and then I'm on the ground, bleeding, a burning pain shooting through my shoulder. I watch Danny drag River away, and lurch to my feet, trying to follow, but he's gone so fast and so is she. I grab the house phone, and dial for an ambulance and the police, before staggering out the front door. I need to find her. I can hear sirens, and some squad cars screech to a halt.

Derek jogs towards me from a black, unmarked car.

"Sam, what's going on? I got a cryptic text from River."

He tries to make me sit down but I shrug him off. "I need to find them!"

"Who, Sam? Come sit down, you're bleeding."

I spin to face him. "Danny shot me and Jasper, Blay's dead, and he took River! He took her! I need to find her." I'm whimpering but I don't give a shit. Danny's gone crazy and kidnapped the woman I love.

"Please help Jasper," I beg.

"The officers are with him, Sam, and the ambulance is just pulling up. I need you to tell me everything you know about Danny, any places you think he would go."

I close my eyes, trying to think. When I open them, I see paramedics rush into the house. One stops and asks to look at my wound but I shrug her off.

"Sam, you need to get medical attention. These things seem minor but can be a lot worse than they look. When I find and bring River home, she's going to need you healthy."

"Fine."

The paramedic cuts my favourite shirt away from my skin, leaving me exposed while she checks the wound.

"The bullet has missed everything vital. It will hurt for a while, but shouldn't leave you with any permanent damage. We need to take you in to get it cleaned and stitched."

Her voice cuts off when two paramedics rush from the back garden with a gurney. A pale, unconscious Jasper lays lifeless on top of it. I push the girl from me and run to Jasper. "Is he going to be okay?"

"He's lost a lot of blood. We need to get him into surgery."

Oh my God.

"Sam, did Danny kill Blaydon?"

I shake my head. "I think he killed himself."

His face pales, his face contorting in grief. He stands, unblinking and I reach up towards him and shove him. "Derek."

His eyes snap to mine. "Will River try to contact you?"

I try to think if River would even have her phone on her, my mind buzzes with images and information, trying to work through everything that's happening. "Maybe if she can escape him."

I rush to my car and grab my phone. I run up the steps to my house. Jasper has the same phone and always leaves his charger plugged into the kitchen wall. I plug my phone into it and wait for some life to show on the screen. When it finally comes on, it signals a message. I hit the voicemail button and put it on speaker.

The message ends and I realise Derek has followed me in.

"She was standing with Blaydon on that decking, fire around her. She was going to kill herself," I whisper in disbelief. My wonderful, beautiful girl was so fucking broken, and I left her twice. I watch a uniformed officer walk into my house and up to Derek.

"One dead body. We found this note in the house addressed to River. It's a suicide note from the brother."

Derek takes the note and reads it, grief shadowing his features again before he says, "I knew something wasn't right with them. I could feel it. I looked into Danny's past. His sister's death was classed as an accident but it's unusual for an eight-year-old to drown. Now his father has gone missing." He sighs. "I should have got her out of there. I could sense something with her. I should have saved her before any of this happened. Now her brother's gone, she may not survive that loss after everything else. She came to me asking questions, being all cryptic. She was going to confess tomorrow. I shouldn't have let her leave."

I walk right up so we we're nose to nose. "I left her with a rapist for four fucking years, and now he's taken her after shooting my best friend and me. Let's not go over who's fucked up the most, let's just find her."

He nods in agreement. "Let's get you to the hospital and get you fixed up."

I don't argue. My shoulder is on fire and I think I'm going to pass out from the pain. I want to welcome the unconsciousness. To let it fade out all the pain I heard in my River's voice, to make it take away the images of Danny stealing her innocence. I want it to take away the guilt that has manifested inside my veins for leaving her all those years ago, but she needs me and if she calls I need to be there to answer. If Derek gets a lead, I have to be there to follow him on it. I need to be awake for when she comes back to me.

Derek drives me to the hospital and charges my phone in his car on the way. I stare at it, willing it to ring but it doesn't. I keep going over everything in my head, everything I know about Danny to try and get a clue to where he would take her. I know he loves her but he's on the crazy train right now and I'm terrified he'll hurt her.

We pull up at the hospital and Derek leads me straight into the back, past the nurse station. "I'll find out what's happening with Jasper. You get sorted out. I'll be back."

I sit on the gurney to wait for the nurse.

"Agent, I heard the coroner is bringing in a Blaydon Kane. Is he any relation to a River Kane?"

I jump from the bed and go to the curtain to listen to what the nurse is saying to Derek.

"Yes, how do you know her?"

"She was here earlier today. We treated her for a head injury. I flagged her chart because the man who came in with her seemed off to me, and then he stole the results to her urine sample."

What the fuck? Why did she have a head injury?

"Why would he steal urine sample results?"

I hear her feet shuffle. "Well, he informed the doctor he's sterile when we asked if Miss Kane could be pregnant, but the test confirmed she *is* pregnant."

She is pregnant, she is pregnant, she is pregnant.

The words were swimming in my mind repeating. My version became unfocused, white dots clouded my view and then I fainted.

CHAPTER TWENTY-SIX
River

I hurt all over. I lift my head and try to focus. My eyesight is blurry and I'm restrained. Oh, God. I'm bound to a wooden rocking chair, my hands and legs tied. My eyes clear enough for the room to come into focus. There's enough light emanating from a few lamps to highlight all the dust particles floating in the air. I want to hold my breath so I don't breathe them in. Clearly no one has been here in a while, and we've disturbed the place. The walls are all wooden; it looks like some type of cabin. There's a soot-covered fireplace. By the cold feel of the place, everything had been left dormant until Danny brought us here, but where is here? The cabin has a couch and a coffee table; it isn't big but there are a couple of doors which lead further inside.

"I love you. I've never loved anyone, but I loved you from the first day I saw you, when Blaydon invited me over. You were thirteen and beautiful." Danny comes closer, startling me, stroking his hand down my cheek. "You only had eyes for Sammy back then, so I waited and watched you blossom. I was determined to have you. You were meant for me."

I shake my head. "No, I wasn't. I was made for Sammy."

His callous laugh sends chills into my spine. "Well, Sammy is dead."

The realisation of everything he took from me crashes into me like a tidal wave of fear, pain and grief. I feel flayed open; raw and bleeding. I'm done, I can't do this anymore.

"Kill me, Danny. Just kill me."

He gasps and grabs my hair, pulling my head back so I can see his face. His eyes are emotionless, void of anything human. "I can't do that. I won't live without you, and I'm not ready to die yet. I've been working on getting us set for life, and in a couple of days, everything will be ready. We're going to be happy."

He's fucking delusional. "Fuck you, Danny. I will never play nice with you. I hate you!" I bawl, tears flooding onto my face. How many tears can a body produce? I feel like I've produced an ocean's worth. Too many for one person to ever shed.

"I fucking hate you. You took everything from me," I choke.

There's no physical pain that can compete with the emotional agony I'm feeling. Every cell in my body cries for what I've lost. My soul is wilted, dying. If you could touch death, you would feel me because I'm truly dead in my spirit, my heart, my soul. I'm nothing but ash inside, burned up and destroyed by the Devil himself. Only he would send such evil to collect me, break me, end me.

He bends down into my face. "Blaydon was fucking weak, so was your mother. Blaydon knew what her death did to you, and he still bled himself dry."

I twist my face from his. "How can you be so cruel? You know the pain I'm feeling," I cry.

He scoffs. "Why wouldn't I? He wasn't my brother."

I narrow my eyes. "But you lost a sister, didn't you?"

He eyes go wide with shock. He paces a few steps, and then stops. "She was a cunt, a drain on my mother. They worshipped that little bitch! They left me home, ill with measles while they took her to a birthday party because she cried to go." He laughs.

"I could have died because she wanted cake and balloons."

I suck at the air to feel my lungs. "You killed her, didn't you?"

He turns his dark eyes on me. "She fell asleep in the bath and slipped under the water. I just kept her there."

Oh my God. "There's something wrong with you, Danny. You're fucking crazy."

"Crazy in love with you, River, and you love me, or you will again."

"As soon as I get the chance, I'm going to kill you or myself," I tell him.

"Then I won't give you the chance. And before you go thinking of killing yourself, you might want to see this." He holds a piece of paper up to me. It's too close; I squint trying to read it. It's from the hospital. "You're pregnant. Congratulations, we're going to be parents."

This can't be happening. Danny can't have children, so that means I'm pregnant with Sammy's baby. Oh, God.

"I can see the cogs turning in that beautiful head of yours. It's a miracle, River. We're having a baby." I shake my head, and he continues, "I'm the only man you've ever been with. I know this crush with Sammy had you confused for a while, but it was just a silly crush. Now we're having a baby, you'll be my wife, and forget all about Sammy and Jasper."

"You're crazy."

Danny grips my face. "Am I, River? Because if you're telling me that's not my baby inside you, I'll rip it from your fucking womb with my bare hands."

I visibly shake with fear, the knowledge of what he was capable off had me terrified that he would carry out everything he threatened. "It is yours, Danny."

"Of course it is. We belong together, you'll see."

CHAPTER TWENTY-SEVEN
Sammy

"You passed out," are the first words from Derek's mouth. "How are you feeling?"

"She's pregnant," I breathe.

He pinches his eyebrows together, putting his fingers to the bridge of his nose. "You heard that, huh? Listen, Sam, I will find her and bring her home. I'm taking a guess that this is your baby?"

Danny can't have kids. River is pregnant with my baby, and he knows. He took her results.

"Where's Jasper?" I ask, ignoring his question.

"He's out of surgery and doing well. His father showed up around twenty minutes ago."

I look down at the gown I'm wearing and the sling over my shoulder.

"They fixed you while you were sleeping." He smiles.

"There is no fixing me."

I try to move but Derek's hand stops me. "You need to get some rest."

"Fuck that, Derek! She's out there somewhere with that maniac, and she's pregnant with my baby."

He holds his hands up. "I get it, Sammy. But we have nothing to go on yet. There are officers at the Kane household.

The remains of her father were just dug up from the garden. It's crazy there. You're better off resting here while we wait for a lead."

"I can't! What if she gets away and comes to the house looking for me? I need to go."

I know I'm being optimistic, but that's all I can be without breaking. I need to believe she will get away from him. I need to believe she's safe.

"Sammy, if you insist on leaving, let me take you."

I appreciate his help, but I wish he would get out there looking for River. I listen as his phone rings, and he swipes the button and puts it to his ear.

"What you got?"

I stare at him, my body on high alert with every face muscle he moves. "Get down to the department. Get Hance to have a look at it, see if we can get anything from it. Okay, keep me informed." He slips the phone back into his pocket. "They found Danny's laptop. They're taking it to our tech department to see what we can get from it."

I rub my hands down my face. Danny's a genius with technology, there's no way they will pass his firewalls.

The drive back to the scene of the crime is tense. Every minute that passes my hopes dwindle. He could have her out of state by now. It's fucking killing me, the thought of never seeing her again.

"Sammy, you ready?"

I look up at Derek, then out of the window. We're home. A coroner's van is parked on the lawn in River's front garden. There's yellow tape bordering around the front gardens, and floodlights set up, highlighting the house. Some people are walking around in white overalls, going back and forth into River's back yard. Police officers keep nosy neighbours and reporters behind the yellow tape.

"Sammy, Sammy!"

Please tell me I'm imagining my mother's voice. I look over at an officer holding my mother back. She's frantically waving her hands at me. Derek gives the officer the okay to let her through and she smirks like she just one upped him. Can she not see the devastation all around? This isn't a time to be smug. She looks a mess. What possesses a woman to give up the love of a good man, and the happiness of a family to dress like she's eighteen, drinks like frat boy and, let's face it, whore herself out for pennies?

"What happened to you?" she asks, poking me in the arm that's held up by the sling. I grunt from the shooting pain she caused to explode in my shoulder, and back away from her. Her face looks like one of those watercolour paintings, the ones where they let the paint bleed well. My mother's make-up is bleeding off her aged face.

"Why are you back?" I ask.

She huffs and crosses her arms like a six-year-old. "So you didn't miss me?"

Is everyone visiting their inner crazy today or what?

"You were only gone five minutes."

She looks around at the carnage. "Five minutes too long by the looks of it. What happened, and who is he?"

She looks in Derek's direction. He's on the phone again, walking towards us.

"Dream on, Mother."

I didn't like the fact that he eye fucked River, but I'm not bitter enough to pretend Derek isn't a good-looking man, and a wealthy one.

"Sam, Danny's car was spotted near Keepers Woods, about one hundred miles from here. Do you know if he has property there, or knows anyone near there?"

My heart is pounding again. I really am going to have heart failure before the day is through.

My mom pipes up "That's where Keith has a cabin. He used to take me there. In fact, that's probably where Keith's been hiding all these years."

Derek and I look at each other. He dials a number on his phone and informs someone to search property in Keith's name. My mother has a wild imagination so she could be blowing smoke up our asses, but if she isn't, then it couldn't be just a coincidence.

"Mom, you better be telling the truth. And just so you know, Keith's back there." I point to River's garden.

Her mouth drops open and she actually fluffs her hair and pulls the front of her top down so her bra spills out the top. "Why would I lie? It was about nine or ten years ago though, so maybe he got rid of it. I don't know. I can't believe he's back, do I look okay?"

"You disgust me. You were still with dad, then! Oh, and you look okay enough to impress a corpse. He never left."

She furrows her brow. "I don't understand."

"He was under that platform River used to dance on, rotting like the scum he was."

She steps back and looks to the activity coming and going from River's garden, and then she bends over and empties her stomach contents. It's all liquid, just like her diet.

"Did his kids kill him?"

I shrug. "Does it matter?"

She's shaking. "He was Jase's dad," she chokes.

My temper is balancing on a razor's edge. I grip her by her scrawny arm and hiss in her face. "You just never stop fucking our lives up, do you? I'm going to pretend you didn't just tell me that. If you ever breathe a word to Jase, or dad, I will kill you."

She scoffs and pulls her arm from my grip. "Your dad already knows."

I blink back the shock of her information. He knows and still keeps Jase with him? I have a new sense of respect for him. Jase needs a stable parent and Dad gives him that, even though he doesn't have to. That's honourable.

I look away from the mess my mother is, and train my eyes on Derek. He still has the phone to his ear. He spins to face me while he replies to whoever is on the phone.

"Transfer the co-ordinates to my GPS. No, don't inform them yet. I don't want rookie cops going in there and ruining our shot to get her out of there safe, if she's in there."

Adrenaline soars through my veins, my legs moving of their own accord towards Derek's car. I feel his hand come down on my one good shoulder.

"I can't let you come, Sammy. Let me go, and I'll bring her home if she's there. I promise."

I swing the passenger door open. "There's not a chance in hell you're going without me, and the more we stand and debate, the more time we waste."

He cusses but doesn't stop me. Nothing will stop me going to her.

"You're a stubborn son of a bitch, you know that?" he grumbles, as he folds his tall frame into the driver's seat.

"I'm definitely the son of a bitch. Did you see my mother?"

He looks out the front windscreen where my mother is wailing about Keith. Anyone would think she cared about him, but I know better. That woman doesn't possess the gene that allows you to care; her heart is ice fucking cold.

Derek pushes buttons on his GPS before pulling out and speeding down the road.

CHAPTER TWENTY-EIGHT
River

I really need to pee. I can't believe he actually left me tied to a chair. The binds are cutting into my skin as I wriggle to try and free my wrists. Every time I move, the stupid chair moves with me, rocking me. I try to stretch my toes, to place them on the floor, but it makes the binds at my ankles burn my skin. My head is pounding from the blow he delivered earlier with the butt of the gun. An hour, he said. But I have no clock. He could never come back for all I know or care. I could rot in this chair, starve to death and it would still be better than him coming back and dragging me off somewhere to live the same shit I've been living the last four years.

I can't just sit here and rot, though. I have an unborn baby growing in my womb. A piece of Sammy I need to protect. Danny can't share my affection, not that he ever had it, but in his twisted mind he really believes I love him. There's no way he would share that love with a baby. God, he killed his sister when she was eight years old. How does someone do that? He was only twelve. Twelve years old, and a murderer. He really fooled Blaydon and me over our father. All this could have been avoided if we had locked the door to prevent Danny's entry and phoned an ambulance. Where would I be if that night had turned out differently? Would I be in school? Or living with Sammy? Would

Danny still be in our lives? Would Blay be here? Would Sammy have gone off to college and met Jasper, or would Jasper be healthy, alive and scoping out the next victim for his crotch to mingle with? Death has plagued my existence. Mom, Dad, Maria, Blaydon, Jasper and my soul mate, Sammy. Is that all I have to offer the life growing inside me? Misery and death? When it comes down to it, if it weren't for me, every one of those people would still be here. Mom killed herself because she couldn't watch the affection my father had for me, and her death started a domino effect. My dad died because Blay was protecting me, and Danny used it as a way to get to me. Maria was Danny's second try at using death to keep me. Blay couldn't take the guilt, and didn't want me to suffer by staying with Danny so he took his own life. Danny shot both Jasper and Sammy because he was jealous that they had my affection. How many more people would die because of me? I need to kill him, otherwise it's just a matter of time before he would hurt the only thing I have left in this world. I'm going to be a mother, and unlike my mother, I won't fail my child.

I feel the blood dripping from my wrist. It hurts like a bitch, but it's making it easier to slip my hand free. I know Danny's been gone longer than an hour. He needed a computer to transfer funds he's stealing from some big organisation. He was boasting about how easy it is to keep taking little amounts that go under the radar but add up immensely, especially over the two years he's been doing it for. Danny is an expert when it comes to computers. He found out straight away that Saunders had been robbing my father blind at K's motors. He re-programmed the whole system so he could monitor all the accounts, and everything I did while I was at work. I don't know what he expected I would be doing. I wish I'd had the guts to book me and Blay a flight, but Blay was dependent on Danny to supply his drugs. I hated that he had such a shit life. Some people should never have children. He was my parents' outlet for their hatred and abuse. My mom never once stopped the beatings. I knew she was afraid, but I would have gladly taken the harsh treatment just so Blay could sleep without fear, without the demons that awaited him once he closed his eyes.

A loud popping rings out into the quiet cabin, followed by a small sob that tears from my throat as pain shoots up my arm. My hand is free but I can't use it. It's limp and swelling fast. I quickly use my other hand and the rope that was used to bind me to make a sling. It's a shabby job, but it will do, and will hopefully stop me from doing any more damage to my wrist. I pry the knots around my ankles and stand. I feel faint, but this is my chance, I have to take it. I rush to the front door and it opens with ease. It's pitch black. The cabin is surrounded by trees; the pathway is overgrown and recently trodden down, which be from Danny coming and going. It's eerily quiet. I'm debating the best route to take. If I use the path, Danny could come back and find me there easily, but if I chance the trees, I could become more lost and risk further injury, even death. Fuck it, I risk death by not taking my chance with the woods. I drop down the stairs and hurry into the woods. Adrenaline pumps through my veins. I stay relatively close to the treeline so I can follow the path, but from the safety of the trees. I hear rustling from the wildlife all around me and fear begins to replace any adrenaline I first had. My wrist is throbbing, my head feels too heavy for my shoulders and my bladder is full. My shoes aren't fit for traipsing through this type of terrain. My heart is attacking my ribcage with every step I take, and bugs are using me as a food supply. My skin itches.

I hear a car then see a slight whisper of light highlight the trees. Panic seizes me. I'm shaking so much I think my bones will crack and shatter to the floor in a million pieces. The light is passing, and before I can make a dash to get away, it's gone. I know it's only a matter of minutes until Danny reaches the cabin and notices I've gone, so I need to make these minutes count. I pick up my pace, running fast and with purpose. I won't stay still and keep being a victim; I'll fight back for me, for Blaydon, for Jasper and Sammy, for my baby.

Branches whip at my face and body, and I stumble a few times. I hear the engine of a car, but no headlights show. Car doors open and close, more than one. My mind is working overtime to keep me sane. Has he picked someone else up? I crouch down low, my breathing sounds so loud in my ears. I place my hand over my mouth to hold the terrifying fear inside myself. I hear a muffled mumbling, then a shriek, calling out my name in the distance. It's Danny, but if Danny is far behind me, who is in the car in front of me? Do I take a chance it's someone who'll help me, or would I be putting them in danger? But who would be out here the middle of nowhere? Oh, God they could be another threat. Danny's voice pierces the night again. He sounds frantic and I run, my body making the decision for me. I clear the trees and plummet down a small drop into a ditch, my head colliding with a small boulder. The sharp pain takes my breath away, and I hear panicked voices coming closer. I force myself to my feet, my hands grasping at grass and rocks to pull myself from the ditch. Blood coats my face, blurring my eyes. I manage to make it from the ditch and run straight into a wall.

A warm wall.

"No, no! No, let me go! Let me go!"

I'm screaming and thrashing my body, trying to free myself.

"Shh, it's okay, River."

I look up into the soft eyes of Derek.

"River! River, oh God, River." Sammy's voice. His scent fuses into me as he pulls me from Derek's arms.

"I'm dreaming," I cry. "I didn't escape, I'm tied to that chair!"

"Quickly, Sammy. Get her into the car, Danny is closing in."

I shake my head. "Is this real, Sammy?"

I pull back from his embrace and notice his arm is in a sling.

"It's real. I've got you, baby."

I go limp.

"Move now!" Derek shouts.

He pulls his gun and takes off up the overgrown trail towards the cabin. Sammy ushers me into the car with him, cradling me into his lap. The silence is deafening until a gunshot rings out, shattering the silence. Sammy moves underneath me, and slips me into driver's seat. The engine gives a low hum in the stillness of the black night. Sammy gets out of the car and I begin to have an anxiety attack fear making my whole body vibrate.

"Please, Sam. Don't go." My hand shakes as I cling to his leg to stop him from leaving the car.

His hand strokes down my cheek. "I swear I won't let him get you, River, but I can't leave Derek out there with Danny. Danny has no humanity left in him. He's a killer and Derek may be injured."

I know he's right, but I'm afraid of losing him again, and Danny taking me back into captivity.

"Lock the doors, and hit the lights if you see Danny coming. Do not hesitate to back the fuck out of here, and don't stop driving until you know can find a police station."

I shake my head as he exits the car and slams the door. I shakily search for the lights and flip them on. A curtailing scream wrenches from me.

Danny is standing in front of the car, pointing a gun at Sammy. Instinct takes over, and my foot and hand work without my knowledge. Before I can blink, the car is revving forward. Danny's body hits the bonnet with a chilling thud.

CHAPTER TWENTY-NINE
Sammy

I rush to River, diving back into the car and shouting, "Drive, River!"

"Is he dead?"

She puts the car in reverse, but I grab her hand to stop her.

"No, go forward, Twink. We need to find Derek, he could be injured."

She pulls the car forward, driving around the still body of Danny.

"Stop!" I yell after a few yards.

Derek is lying on his stomach, motionless. I jump from the car and rush to him, turning him. There's blood seeping from a wound on his back. I roll him onto his side and check his pulse. It's weak, but he still has one. I drag him to the car and use every last piece of strength I have to tackle his large frame into the back seat.

"Turn the car around, Twink. Let's get out of here."

She struggles with the wheel, using her free hand and her shoulder to turn it. "Are you in pain, baby? Do you want me to drive?" She shakes her head no. Danny's still there when we pass him. I debate getting out and picking up his gun to make sure he never gets back up, but I don't want the evil in him to crawl inside me. I'm not like him. I couldn't end another life and live with myself, even someone who deserved it.

Derek had called for backup once we first found the trail that led to the cabin so I know they'll arrive soon and take Danny into custody, if he's alive.

"Is Derek going to be okay?" River's voice is so timid. I can see the break in her; the cracks in her psyche are there in her face, in her clouded stormy eyes.

"It's over, baby. We'll get Derek fixed up and get you looked at."

I specifically didn't say get her "fixed" because like me, she can't be fixed, but we could be broken together, and fill the cracks that are left from such a fucked up life.

"I'm pregnant," she whispers.

A faint smile lifts my lips. "And you will be an amazing mother. I'll try every day to deserve you both."

She chokes on a sob. Headlights light up the distance and I blow out a thankful breath.

ELEVEN MONTHS LATER
Sammy

Derek comes into the front room with a takeout box nearly as big as the coffee table.

"Pizza."

Jasper approaches River where she's sitting, curled into a ball on the armchair. He places a mug down, steam billowing from the surface, sending a coffee aroma into the air. "Mmm, thank you." She smiles.

"Beer." He grins at me, holding up a six pack.

We had moved into Derek's mansion at his suggestion. I know he felt protective over River for reasons I wasn't entirely sure about. It has to do with her losing Blay; he seems to share a similar loss, but I've never questioned him on it. I'm just grateful for everything he's done for us. I didn't really have any place to take River when she refused to return to our houses. Ghosts haunted her there. She cried for an hour straight when I told her Jasper was okay, one less death for her to blame herself for. The acts of Danny have imprinted onto her soul. She carries the burden, wears it in her actions. It's there in her eyes when she laughs and then catches herself, like she feels wrong for feeling anything other than grief and guilt. The only time I see glimpses of peace, glimpses of the tropical eyes that looked at me through the hole in the fence is when she's holding our son, Michael. She named him after the Archangel. She said the angels must have been protecting him in the womb for him to be able to survive the trauma she went through while he was so fragile. She wouldn't listen when I told her it was her resilience and courage that protected him. Michael Blaydon is our son's name. He's beautiful, and loved not just by me and River, but by Jasper and Derek too. I think he represents that from the rubble of destruction can come a second chance. A soul full of possibilities and hope. River still suffers from the after effects of that night, and the memories that plague her dreams. She's terrified that Danny will come for her. When the agents got to the cabin that night, they didn't recover a body. He was gone. They combed the area for two days, but he wasn't found. If I'd known he wouldn't be caught, I would have done things differently. If I'd have known how badly River would have anxiety attacks and nightmares, thinking he was coming for her, I would have taken his life that night. My girl is put together with sticky tape at the moment, and I want him to pay for his cruelty. I want to give River a small piece of justice. I want to fill her cracks and mend her soul. That's

Another reason Derek insisted we stay with him. He has extra security measures put in place at his mansion to make River feel as safe as possible. We've all grown close, bound together by a shared trauma. Jasper decided to move in with us rather than go home with his dad to heal. The place is big enough for us not to get under each other's feet. If anything, I'm grateful to have him here. We need each other. We're a family of broken parts, but together we work like a jigsaw. We all fit together to create a perfect picture, but just like any jigsaw, the cracks are still visible. My dad and I spoke about Jase being Keith's. He told me he raised Jase because he loves me, and Jase may not be his, but he's a part of me which meant he was part of him. Hearing that helped me in so many ways. It helped mend the small boy who still lives inside of me, hoping for my parents love and approval. River was shocked when I told her Jase is her half-brother. She said he's a gift from the wreckage our parents wreaked, but agreed to keep it from him so he can live without knowing the monster he came from.

River inherited K's Motors and I run it, so when I'm at work, Jasper stays home with River. She hardly ever leaves the mansion, she fears leaving the safety she feels here. Derek pays a therapist to come to the house to see her, and she's improving in small steps.

"I'm going up to get some sleep before the little guy wakes up for a bottle," she says, bringing me from my thoughts. I drop the slice of pizza I'm holding and stand.

"Yeah, I'm going to …" I can't think of an excuse, and blurting out that I'm going to ravish my girl's amazing body would be too much information, but the smirk all over Jasper's face and the eye roll from Derek tells me an excuse is not necessary. I make a quick exit, tapping River's gorgeous ass as I rush her to the stairs. She chuckles and it's the most beautiful sound I've ever heard. I chase her into our room, closing the door and pinning her sexy frame against the wall, my mouth devouring hers.

"I love you, baby," I breathe into her skin. I slip my shirt over my head dropping it to the floor.

My hands roam every delicious curve of her body; I feel her pulse racing with every needy breath she takes. This is the only time she allows herself to completely let go, knowing that I'm right there to catch her, and follow her into ecstasy.

"Make love to me, Sammy."

God, she makes my dick throb when she says shit like that. I pop the buttons open on my jeans and push them from my body, leaving me bare and ready to be inside my women. Just as I strip her sundress from her shoulders, Michael starts to cry; the sound echoing in the baby monitors around the house. I sigh and released the hold I have on her dress, slipping it back into place. Static, then Jasper's voice speaks from the monitor. "Uncle Jasper has this one, guys. You carry on getting it on …I mean getting some sleep."

His chuckle carries down the hall from Michael's nursery. My eyes find the lustful gaze of River's, and she leans forward, taking my bottom lip into her mouth and biting down. She's so hot when she's turned on. No one can light me up like her. I strip her from her dress and panties; worshipping the beauty on display for me. I trace my lips over her soft skin, taking her pert nipple into my mouth sucking gently. Her moans feed my need for her.

"Touch your tits, baby. Let me see you please yourself while I taste your amazing pussy."

Her breath catches in her throat. River likes me giving her commands. I drop to my knees in front of my goddess. Her aroused scent sends me into frenzy. I lean forward to swipe my tongue into the crease of her pink, moist pussy. She tastes the perfect blend of sweet and sin; it's like nothing else I've ever tasted. It's unique to her, and it brings out the alpha male in me. She's not only beautiful, she's sexy. Her figure rivals any underwear model; she rivals any Hollywood starlet, and her hunger and sex drive rivals any male.

"Keep doing that, baby. Pinch those nipples," I command her, while opening her pussy with my thumb and index finger, my eyes committing every detail of her to memory because I swear every time I get between her thighs, her pussy gets more beautiful.

"Oh, God, Sammy! More, more!"

Her hands drop from her nipples into my hair. Her hips push her closer on to my lips. I nip and suck on her clit, sliding two fingers into her wet depths. Her pussy squeezes me while her orgasm rips through her. I slip my fingers from her and use my tongue to dip into her hot core, soaking up everything she has to offer. Her hands grip and tug my hair, forcing my head away from her. I look up into her hooded gaze; her lips crushing down on mine.

"I love tasting myself on you."

I wrap my arms around her naked ass, squeezing in it my palms, sliding my hands up her body as I get to my feet.

I take her lips with mine, making love to her mouth with my tongue. Gripping her thighs and lifting her, I slide straight into her welcoming heat.

"I love you" She pants. Her fevered body pinned to mine as I rock into her with slow. Deep. Thrusts.

"Your mine Twink, I love you so much" I breathe against her lips, my mouth capturing every gasp that leaves her.

I feel her heat all around me, squeezing me, surrendering herself to my love. I walk us to the bed sitting down so she's straddling me.

"Make love to me baby" I whisper.

She lifts her hips and slowly rotates them, dropping her ass back down to accept me fully inside her. Her hands reach forward to link with mine: her head tipping back pushing her chest forward. I swirl my tongue around her nipple, her body thrusting more urgently against me.

"I love you, I love you" She calls out as she contracts all around me with her release, demanding mine in return.

I wake up to an empty bed. This is not unusual. I know I'll find her curled up on the armchair in Michael's room, so I shower and get ready for work before going to find her. Just like I predicted, there she is, asleep in front of his crib.

"Hey, buddy," I coo as I pick him up to cradle him in my arms. His pouty mouth is all River, his colouring is all me. His dark velvet to touch hair had all the nurses fussing over him when he was born. Everyone thinks their own child is beautiful, but we really did good with him. He's perfection, just like his mommy. He's thirteen weeks old now, and River has been cleared to dance by the doctors so I'm going to surprise her with the studio today. She has no idea I bought it. I had some work done to bring it back to its best, and had the name changed. I'm hoping this will give her something to put herself into; give her something to feel positive and passionate about again.

"Hey," she murmurs in a sleepy tone.

I smile at my gorgeous girl. "Hey, baby."

I place Michael back in his crib before I pull River up into my arms. Her sweet coco scent makes me feel grounded.

"I have a surprise for you today. Get dressed, baby. I'll get Michael ready."

She looks at me with suspicion, making me chuckle. "It's a good surprise," I tell her, tapping her ass and ushering her from the room.

CHAPTER THIRTY

River

My image reflects back at me in the mirror, the small scar from my fall that night a reminder on the outside of how many scars are on the inside. I live in a constant state of awareness; awareness of what I lost at the hand of Danny, and the fear he will come for me. Sammy says he more than likely died in the woods. He was injured and not familiar with those woods. I know different, though. I feel it deep in my soul. I know by the ghosts that haunt me that can't be at peace until he has paid for his crimes. Burying Blaydon was the hardest thing I've ever done, and even after eleven months, two days, and three hours, part of me stayed there at his grave, wishing things had been different. You can't change what's already passed, you can only prepare and be ready to prevent it happening again. I'm scared the fear has manifested inside me into a living being, making me stronger, making me ready to end him when he does come for me.

I slip into casual jeans and a tank top, and twist my hair into a messy knot, securing it with a band. I forgo make-up, just spraying light perfume so I'm not a complete mess. I descend the stairs to see Jasper strapping Michael to his chest in his baby carrier. I quirk a brow. "What do you think you're doing?"

He turns to face me, a grin spreading wide on his face. "Pussy patrol."

Sammy slaps him round the head. "Jasper's taking Michael to the park so I can show you your surprise."

This piques my interest. I'm picturing more of the delights of last night. Sammy sees the lust-filled look on my face and smirks. "Not that kind of surprise, Twink."

"So, Jasper is taking our son to the playground even though he's way too young to even use it?"

I know why he's really going to the playground, and I must admit Jasper looks so cute with a baby strapped to his chest. His playboy looks and mannerisms combined with his devotion to our son is a sure fire way to get him laid.

"The playground is for me. It's my dick's playground, full of bored housewives and single parents, all frustrated and needing a release. I'll take numbers and work my way through them, giving them the best night of their lives."

I take the last step until I'm next to Jasper and give him a deadly glare. "So you're using my son to pick up easy women, rather than spending time with him because you love him?"

He looks offended and shakes his head. "No. I love him so I'm spending time with him. The easy women are just a bonus. This little guy is a babe magnet. I'm just using the perks which is my right as uncle."

Sammy chuckles and slaps Jasper around the head again. "Get out of here before she starts un-strapping him and bans you from ever seeing him again."

Jasper gasps. "She wouldn't."

My eyes narrow on him. He quickly walks to the door and exits before I can say anything. Sammy closes his arms around me from behind, whispering in my ear. "You are a devil woman, and I love you."

I turn in his embrace so I can kiss his soft lips.

"Mmm, don't get me excited, baby. I want to show you your surprise first." He winks and ushers me out the front door.

We drive into the car park of Bella's. I haven't been here since it sold, but I've driven past it with longing. I miss the escape I used to find here. No one knows who bought it or what they're going to do with it. It hasn't been open since it sold, though, so hope dwindled for it remaining as a dance studio.

I let my eyes take in the new name and my heart begins to pitter patter in a low, steady beat. *Twinkle Toes Dance Studio.*

Tears well in my eyes. "Sammy, what is this?"

He lets out an awkward laugh. "It's your dance studio. I bought it for you. I just wanted to wait until you were ready to come back here."

My tears fall freely. I feel so much love inside me for this man, I'm afraid my body can't contain it, or that he's going to be snatched away from me like everyone else in my life.

"Talk to me, baby. You're making me nervous."

I unbuckle my seat belt and crawl into his lap. "Thank you for giving me back a part of me, Sammy, for mending the broken parts of me and loving me in spite of them. I love you. This is so amazing. *You're* so amazing."

He crushes his lips to mine. "You're amazing, River, and I love you. The whole you, the broken you; every shattered piece. And I will fill all those cracked pieces with the love I feel for you, until you feel whole again."

My tears spill on to my cheeks and Sammy wipes them with the pads of his thumbs. "I may never be whole Sammy."

He smiles. "Then we'll stay broken together."

He reaches into his jeans pocket and pulls out a black velvet ring box. My eyes widen.

"I have only ever loved you, River. You were my Twinkle

Toes. You were the light in my darkness, you made me feel loved. You gave it freely when people that should have offered it to me didn't. You gave me my son who I will love and support with every fibre of my being, even when Jasper tries to turn him into a whore." I shake my head furiously, making him laugh, and he continues, "I want forever with you. I've always wanted forever with you. Please make me complete. Marry me?"

I grip him to me so tightly I'm scared he will fracture. "Yes, yes, yes. You're it for me, Sammy. It's always been you."

He nods his head, looking relieved his eyes sparkle and he lets out a breath in a rush. "I'm taking you to celebrate. I thought you could come back here tomorrow so you can get reacquainted with the place on your own?"

I scoot back into my own seat. "That would be perfect, thank you."

He takes the ring from the box. "Let me put this on you, baby."

I hold my hand out to him and he takes it, bringing it to his lips before he slips the ring in place It's stunning; a princess cut, not too big. Elegant, perfect, just like him.

The drive home is filled with talking about how quickly he can get me down the aisle. I have no desire to wait or have some big wedding where most of the chairs will sit empty. My family lives under our one roof, so the wedding will be just us. We pull up onto the drive, but Sammy doesn't exit when I do. I poke my head back in the door.

"Go make yourself feel gorgeous, baby. I need to pop to work quickly, then I'll be back to get you."

I smile and rush inside. Jasper isn't back yet, and Derek is working so I began stripping myself from my clothes on my way up the stairs. I slip out of my underwear and search my dresser for my fancy black lace panty set. I pull my hair from its messy knot, shaking the strands free. Walking into my wardrobe, I scan the contents, looking though my dresses.

"The white one. I love you in white."

Ice cold dread works its way up my spine. *Was that real or have I finally snapped?* A hand on my shoulder and the change in atmosphere warns me that he's real. I spin my body around, not wanting my back to him in case he hits me over the head with something.

"How did you get in here?"

Danny's dark eyes bore into me. He looks unkempt. He has a beard, and his hair is longer. His clothes are dirty, but those eyes they are the same. "Is that what you have to ask me after not seeing me for so long? Have you not missed me?"

"How did you get in here?" I repeat, trying to buy time.

"The security is good, but so am I. Beautiful, I can breach anything. I got past the firewalls in an hour to get the codes for the alarm system and to turn off the cameras. Simple, really."

The phone rings, startling me. Danny's eyes go to the bedside table where the phone lays. I take his distraction as an opportunity, and dart past him, but he's quick, and grabs out for me. I use one of the self-defence technics Derek taught me. Using the palm of my hand I jab upwards at his nose, blood explodes from the impact. I lift my knee, connecting with his crotch, and he doubles over. I turn to run, but he reaches out, grabbing my calf. I fall down with a hard thud. I turn onto my back and kick at Danny's hands and face.

"River, stop it!" he roars.

I manage to break his hold and scamper across the floor to my dresser. I pull out the gun Derek had bought me and trained me to use. I feel Danny behind me. "Beautiful?"

I turn and point the gun right on his forehead, pulling the trigger. The loud, sharp ring makes my ears pop and the kickback jolts my body. I watch him fall to the floor, his blood spraying over me like shower of justice. He deserves to pay for his sins in blood. I can't lower the gun, I just hold it over him.

CHAPTER THIRTY-ONE
Sammy

I get to the lot and call Stevie to the office. Stevie's a loyal employee. He's worked here longer then I've lived so I trust him, and he was the right choice when I needed a co-manager.

"What's up, son?"

I smile. "I have to take my fiancée out to celebrate. I want to take a few days off."

His returning grin makes me smile bigger. I'm acting like a huge pussy, but I didn't give a shit. We fucking earned this happiness, and nothing can take my smile of my face.

"Well, it's about time. Go, take as long as you need. Give my congratulations to the little lady."

I shake his hand and pat his back when he embraces me. My cell chirping stops me from becoming anymore of a pussy by gushing about how happy I am. I see Derek's name and hit accept.

"Hey, man, she said yes," I say, proudly.

"Is she with you, Sammy?"

The anxiety in his voice has the hairs on the back of my neck standing on end.

"I dropped her at home about thirty minutes ago, why?"

He exhales. "Are Jasper and Michael at the house?"

I start to panic and I'm already making my way across the lot to my car. "No, why, Derek? What's happening?" I'm full on shouting now.

"Someone took the cameras out and breached the firewall to the alarm system. I'm about twenty minutes out, I've call a squad car to go check it out. Sammy, it could be nothing."

He tries to sound reassuring, but I can hear the worry in his voice.

"It's him," is all I say before ending the call and dialling the house. No answer. I try her cell, but get nothing. Burning rage is like lava in my veins. If he's taken her, I won't be able to cope. The burn of tears laces my lashes and I dial Jasper's cell.

"Hey, man! So, is she off the market for good or do I still have a chance?" His mood is light and I hear kids' laughter in the background so I know he's still out which means Michael is safe.

"Don't go back to the house until I call you," I tell him and he chuckles.

"No problem sealing the deal, eh?"

I don't respond. I throw the phone in the passenger seat and speed all the way to the mansion. I'm not even sure I wait for the car to stop before I'm out and racing into the house.

"River?"

Nothing. I race into the front room, frantically searching for her. I run up the stairs, checking each room. I come to ours and freeze. Standing in her underwear, covered in blood, my Twinkle Toes. At her feet was Danny, a seeping bullet hole in his forehead, blood covering his mouth and chin from what looked like a nose injury. My girl is holding a gun, pointed at the still form below her. I approach her with caution, not wanting to startle her.

"Baby, it's me, Sammy."

"I won't be his victim anymore, Sammy."

Her voice shakes as she speaks. I hear a flurry of activity from downstairs and Derek bursts into the room. He surveys the scene and relaxes his tense stance.

"It's okay, River. He's dead. Pass me the gun, sweetheart."

She turns her eyes to me. "I couldn't let him take me, Sammy."

I reach for her, and Derek takes her gun.

"I know, baby. You did good. You did so good. It's over."

She begins to shake from the sob that rips from her chest. "It's really over."

EPILOGUE
FIVE YEARS LATER

"So Jasper's bringing her to dinner?"

I'm in shock. Jasper has never had a serious girlfriend. He is the definition of a playboy, so when Sammy told me he's getting serious with a girl he met, I didn't believe him.

"Yes, he wants you to meet her, which is his test, by the way, to see if she can win your approval."

I laugh at my delicious husband. "She doesn't need my approval."

He cocks an eyebrow. "Jasper puts your opinion above anyone else's. It's a test, but he must really like this girl to be bringing her to family dinner night, so go easy on them."

His hands are stroking my stomach, his head resting just above my panty line.

"Do we have time, baby?" he asks, dropping his hand into my panties.

I moan when he flutters his kisses over my aching clit and down to my entrance.

"Mmm, so warm and wet, baby," he groans.

"Daddy!" Michael bellows as he comes running in. Sammy's hand quickly retreats as do his lips. He kisses my growing bump and sits up to catch our son as he launches himself at him.

"Hey, little man."

Sammy begins his usual morning tickle attack and Michael's giggles float around the room, making me feel content. It took tragedy and heartbreak to get us here, but things have been good for the last few years. I still see my therapist once a month as nightmares sneak up on me every now again, mainly when Michael's features and colouring begin to change. Sammy tells me I'm paranoid and he refuses to have DNA test done. He says Michael is his son, end of. We moved out of Derek's when we got married, five months after I shot and killed Danny. I felt parts of myself heal that day. I took my vows. I was Sammy's, and he was mine.

The dance studio is doing fantastic. I have some great girls who teach with me and help manage the place, which I will need more than anything now I'm expecting our second child. I'm four months pregnant, and Sammy shed a tear when I told him. He's an amazing parent, despite the fact he had no one to learn from. He was just born to be a daddy. His mother is AWOL, but we have nothing to do with her anyway, so she can stay that way. In our minds, she died along with any ties we had to those houses and my parents. Our new house is a beautiful two story four bedroom dream house that Sammy bought us after selling his old home. I refused to sell mine. Instead, I had it demolished. No one should ever have to live in that tomb. We still all gather at Derek's on a Sunday for family dinner night, and Jasper still lives there. He and Derek have a bachelor bromance going on when he isn't at my place, making me cook for him. He isn't just Sammy's best friend, he and I have a great friendship. I adore him, and I seem to be the only female he values. Derek is like a brother to me and Sammy both; his love and protection is invaluable to me and we spend as much time together as a family as we can. He has no other family, just like us.

"Come here, little man, we have some exciting news to tell you." Sammy's voice penetrates my memories. I sit up and pull Michael on to my lap. He's five years old now.

"So, how would you feel about having a little brother or sister?" I ask him.

He looks to Sammy. "Will you still love me?"

Sammy pulls him from my lap and sits him on his own. "Of course. You're Daddy's little buddy, and having a new baby brother or sister won't change that. We have plenty of love to share with you both." He nuzzles Michael's neck. I slip from the bed and pull on a robe. "Come on, buddy, let's go make you some breakfast and talk some more, okay?"

He jumps from the bed. "Okay."

Sammy smiles and follows us out of the room. I turn to smile at them when I got to the top of the stairs, but feel hands shove me forward. I tumble down the stairs, managing to brace myself and grabbing the rail to stop myself from descending the full stairs. Sammy rushes down to pick me up, shock written all over his face. We both turn our heads upwards to see Michael.

"I don't want to share your love."

The air leaves my lungs. I'm looking at my baby. I'm staring into his father eyes. Danny's eyes, his eyes…

THE END

Keep reading for the sneak peek at the prologue for
The Broken Parts Of Us........ Jasper's book

PROLOGUE
JASPER

Danny's glare had solidified my insides; I couldn't move. People assume if someone pulled a gun on them they would wrestle it away and use it against the
person, or they would say a big 'fuck you' and accept the bullet.

We're all fucking heroes in the what if game, but I can tell you, I am not a wimp, I can hold my own in a fight, I don't shy away from conflict and I'll have my friends back in any situation. But when a gun is pointed at you by a mad man you revert back to being a little boy. Your body seizes, fear holds you hostage, your life flashes before your eyes and you start preying that you will get to see the people you love again, even if there are only two of them.

I might be a go lucky man whore but I'm still a person. I have wants and ambitions. I don't want to die for no other reason than someone going of the deep end. I want to live, experience life. You run scenarios through your head; maybe if I kicked his legs out from under him? Maybe if I try to communicate with him? Maybe if I beg? But for me, my body wouldn't comply with any of these things. I was in shock! My best friend's girl, my friend River was holding her dead brother, a man I had shared beers with and her crazy ass boyfriend, who fucking hated me was talking about me and Meadow like we were an item while holding a gun on me.

......*Then he shot me*......

So every person that says they would do this or that, live in my motherfucking shoes. You don't know what you would do or how it will change you, until you're looking down the barrel of a gun with a crazy mother fucker holding the trigger.

ABOUT THE AUTHOR

When not lost in her mind of characters Ker can be found reading or spending time with family.

She has a passion for music, attending concerts with her sister and enjoying the occasional nights out with girlfriends.

She can also be found having in-depth chats about book boyfriends on face book in some amazing groups and blogs.

For news, updates and teasers come join me on Facebook
Author Facebook Page
Email here at
kerryduke34@gmail.com

Add me on Goodreads
The Broken Goodreads

ACKNOWLEDGEMENTS

I want to start with a huge THANK YOU to Dirty Hoe's book blog for giving me my first review, I almost cried hehe. For loving the story and giving me amazing support. For hosting the Blog tour, you girls really went all out and there isn't enough I can say to tell you how grateful I am.

To my wonderful beta readers, I really got lucky with you ladies, Christina, Stephanie, Nikki, Tara, Leah, Penny. To Steph Lewis my hard core beta and Kim Brown, Vikki Ryan, you girls are awesome. Thank you for loving this story.

Thank you to Kyra Lennon for editing The Broken, you did amazing job!.

To black firefly for all the support.

Thank you to my mum for her support. My family for me ignoring them to lose myself with Sammy and River.

To all the blogs that support indie authors, you guys rock. To rockers & bikers romance page, although this isn't about rock stars, Donna you've been really supportive and a friend thank you. A big thanks to Fictional mens room for book ho's, everyone in this group are amazing and supportive and kept me sane these last weeks before publishing.

Thank you to Ari from Cover it! Designs. You did an incredible job helping me with the perfect cover. You're crazy talented.

D.H Sidebottom for just being on my wave length and letting me ask you questions, I love your characters and books, you're awesome.

Pepper Winters for just being lovely, answering my questions and being supportive, I adored Tears of Tess you're an amazing writer.

To all the Authors that inspire me and the passionate readers who loved the teasers and couldn't wait to devour The Broken. This is a dream come true thank you everyone who has been a part of it.

*Sneak Peek into the International Bestselling Series
"Monsters in the Dark"
by
Pepper Winters*

Tears of Tess
Available now
Amazon
Amazon.co.uk
Barnes and Noble

A.M.A.Z.I.N.G. Newest addition to my 'favorites' list!!! Swooning
Over Books*

6 STARS - BEST BOOK I'VE READ THIS YEAR! Hook Me
Up Book Blog*

6 out of 5 BRANDING stars!!! THE BEST BOOK OF 2013!
Prima Donna*

PROLOGUE

Three little words.

If anyone asked what I was most afraid of, what terrified me, stole my breath, and made my life flicker before my eyes, I would say three little words.

How could my perfect life plummet so far into hell?

How could my love for Brax twist so far into unfixable?

The black musty hood over my head suffocated my thoughts, and I sat with hands bound behind my back. Twine rubbed my wrists with hungry stringed teeth, ready to bleed me dry in this new existence.

Noise.

The cargo door of the airplane opened and footsteps thudded toward us. My senses were dulled, muted by the black hood; my mind ran amok with terror-filled images. Would I be raped? Mutilated? Would I ever see Brax again?

Male voices argued, and someone wrenched my arm upright. I flinched, crying out, earning a fist to my belly.

Tears streamed down my face. The first tears I shed, but definitely not the last.

This was my new future. Fate threw me to the bastards of Hades.

"That one."

My stomach twisted, threatening to evict empty contents. Oh, God.

Three little words:

I was sold.

Made in the USA
Charleston, SC
05 May 2014